The Chronicles of Nightfire, Texas

Also by Glenn Slade Clark, Jr.

Novels and Collections

Cry, Wolf

The Great Debate

Metrognomes: The Shaman's Apprentice

Short Fiction E-Books

The Rainbow-Colored Sheep

The Ghost in the Olive Grove

Aries' Cage

Ooga Booga Stories:
Night Light
Night Light II

Metrognomes:
Music of the Metrognomes
Worse than a Gremlin

Dr. Coffee's Pill

Breath

Hollow Jane

The Escapist

The Gift

The Legends of Nod

The Briar Patch Evangelist

Benches

Scarecrow

The Christmas Spirit

Volume I

The Vampire Murders

Glenn Slade Clark, Jr.

2013

The Chronicles of Nightfire, Texas, Volume I:
The Vampire Murders

First Collected Edition: February 2013

Published by Clark Ink, LLC.

This novella was originally serialized from 2000 to 2001 as *The Chronicles of Nightfire, Texas* #1-3.

Cover art by Ryan Fagan.

ISBN-10: 1-61815-086-3
ISBN-13: 978-1-61815-086-8

For Ryan Fagan;
my cousin, my friend, the voice in my head, who always gets what I'm doing, no matter how bizarre.

CONTENTS

CHAPTER 1
HOMECOMING

Nightfire, Texas
October 9, 1974
2:22 A.M.

"Ah. Home at last." Valen took in a deep breath of the air in Nightfire, Texas. Remembering. He put down his bags momentarily and turned around with a worried expression on his face. He spoke to his taller friend who stood on the opposite side of the little stone, Texas-shaped sign that read:

WELCOME TO NIGHTFIRE THE BEST KEPT SECRET IN TEXAS

"Julius," he said, "are you sure this is the best idea?"

"Absolutely. They'll never be able to get to you here. This is the safest place in Texas, as far as they're concerned." He chuckled to himself. "As far as I'm concerned too, for that matter. I can already smell it, ever so faintly. You'll be safe in Nightfire for as long as it takes."

Valen seemed to ponder that. He then met Julius eye to eye. "Yes, I'm sure of that, but...I meant..."

Julius, knowing Valen as well as he did, understood what his friend was thinking, and a look of concern fell over him like a shadow. He stood for a moment, looking like a statue of some ancient god, his short, blonde hair barely blowing in the slight breeze. "No," he said at last. "You don't need to worry about the people here either. It's been too long. Surely you're forgotten by now." Julius smiled. "And even so, it's not as though you're going in alone."

Valen locked eyes with the beast at Julius' side, and he smiled in spite of his apprehension. "What's the matter, girl? Not anxious to leave your Uncle Jules?" Valen looked up to see Julius rolling his eyes with amusement. The smile took on a somber tone. "I'm going to miss you, Julius. You've been a good friend. I'll stay in touch. Let you know how things are going."

Julius nodded wanly. "Good. See that you do. But you'd better get going. It shouldn't be too hard to find your way in. The old Alexas mansion is still intact and in good shape, so I've heard. It may be in need of some minor repairs, but that's not bad, considering how long it's been unoccupied."

Valen nodded again, the wind a bit stronger now, as it caressed his long, dark brown hair. He reached into his pocket and removed a hairband, with which he easily pulled his elegant, wavy locks back into a ponytail. "I'm pleased to hear it." Valen looked over his shoulder at the town that awaited him, then he turned back to his traveling companion, with whom he was about to part ways. He chuckled with a fond recollection. "I wonder if this place has made up its mind yet. Nightfire's always been somewhere on the line between a town and a city. Somewhere between urban and rural. Either way, this town's all Texas. That's one thing I've always been certain of. Take care of yourself, Julius."

"I've lasted this long, haven't I?" He grinned. "Godspeed, Valentinus. I'll keep you in my thoughts and prayers. And I'll send the rest of your things shortly."

Valen gave Julius one final farewell nod, then he turned, stooped, and picked up his luggage. "Come along, Raksha."

The wolf leapt eagerly from Julius' side, as she went to join her master. The pair walked into town, and Julius watched them until they had left his sight.

Mary Jean Donavan, better known to the people of Nightfire, Texas as "Mary the Witch," wandered out of her little, silver trailer home at the edge of town. It was the dead of night, and all was quiet to the ear, but there were great, distressing sounds to be heard by any with the sixth sense with which to hear them. Something was not right. Something ominous had begun, and Mary Jean was restless. She needed to know what it was.

Mary Jean was fifty-two years old, and a hermit by choice. She had a very strong psychic gift, and she had eventually decided that living on the outskirts of town in a trailer home, seeing people only when it was for business, was much better than making actual friends. It was much better to see the fate of a business acquaintance than to see the fate of someone for whom she actually cared. And that's all there was to Mary Jean really, at this point. She saw precious little of her sister now, and even less of her sister's husband and daughter. Sadder still, she almost never saw her son, but she knew that he was on a worthy path, and that made it easier to cope with. Besides, she preferred things as they were. It was so much easier just being alone. And as for her business, it all came quite naturally. Mary Jean told fortunes. She read palms and cards for show, but she could always see the future, at least in part, simply by gazing into a person's eyes. The people of Nightfire would mock her and tell outlandish stories about her, she knew. But, each in turn would come to her, seeking her insights; and Mary Jean would never lead them astray.

She listened for a sign. She watched for it under light of the stars. Nothing seemed unusual. Nothing out of place, save for that unsettling feeling that something was not right.

Something ominous was in the works. Then again, it seemed to her that there was always something ominous in Nightfire. Sometimes, Mary Jean found herself thinking that surely the town must be damned. The land upon which it had been built, or the very town itself, must have been cursed at some point in its history. But the past was not her business, so she had never taken the time to research it. Though, many a teenager had claimed to have seen the ghost at the Witch's Tree—a famous tree from whence a witch had allegedly been hanged long ago—most dismissed it as an urban legend. Even to Mary Jean, it was simply an intriguing possibility.

Her eyes caught something moving on the wind. She reached out and pulled it from the air to examine it closer. "Wolf's hair. How strange." As far as she knew, there were no wolves in Nightfire. Just then, a much more dynamic image caught her watchful gaze, fluttering through the dark night, taking a position on a bare tree branch not far from her at all. Suddenly, the feeling in her gut gave way to knowledge. "Butterfly that flies by night. In October no less. Yes." She nodded to herself, before making the sign of the cross over her chest. "Vampire." She backed away, never letting the colorful insect out of her sight, until she was safely back inside of her home, behind locked door and under the protection of many a magical trinket.

Twenty-three-year-old Raymond Don breathed a sigh of relief, as he fell down to the bed, clutching the hotel towel with which he had just been drying his hands and face. Now that he had buried his little treasure and cleaned away any evidence of his digging, he could at last take some time to process all that he'd been through, and how he'd been led back to Nightfire after so many years of traveling the globe. It seemed to Ray that he'd been everywhere. Everywhere except Vietnam. But the Vietnam conflict was over. President Ford, just under a month ago, had offered amnesty to all of the draft-dodgers and deserters of the armed forces, under the condition that they serve in a civil capacity for two years. Ray could handle that. It wasn't Ray's style, and he actually felt that the amnesty should be unconditional, but he didn't have much choice. He'd needed to get far away from Europe. He'd needed to go home, and Ford's unpopular, conditional amnesty offer had made his retreat possible. So what were two years? He was young enough still not to be fazed by such things.

Ray was by no means a Hippie. He liked to consider himself a stronger breed of rebel. He had no use for tripping out and running around stark naked in front of all his heavily sedated friends singing about peace. He was more about control. Ray had torn up his draft papers, because, like the Hippies, he didn't believe in the war. However, unlike the Hippies, Ray didn't see standing against an order to kill and die for a cause that wasn't his own as an excuse to waste away his life and destroy his mind. Ray had a sharp mind, and he was a seeker—always on the prowl for things he wasn't supposed to know, always getting into trouble. The world was too full of places to see, things to learn and do. Why would anyone want to sit around and drop acid all day? It seemed a terrible waste to Ray.

On the other hand, it was his natural tendency to uncover things he wasn't supposed to, his natural tendency to get himself into trouble, that had sent Ray running home again after years of adventure. He refused to regret the way that things had gone. He would make up for the stories he couldn't tell with the abundance of stories that he could. He had been so many places and seen so many things. He especially couldn't wait to tell his friend Elizabeth Krandall all about it. He felt certain that he'd seen and done far more than even she now. Especially with his last little exploit. But he wasn't going to think about that one. Not now. Not for a while. Maybe later, when he could cash in on it. It was something that for now he *had* to forget. Not only because of the danger that might come to him, but also for the fact that thinking on the things he'd learned, the ancient secrets he'd managed to uncover, caused him to literally go into screaming fits. He knew he'd need to think on it. He'd need to let it all out, process. But for now he would ignore it. It was literally buried where no one would think to look, and he would have access at any time. He would forget it and pretend that it hadn't happened for a little while. He would wait until Lee made contact. If Lee got out okay, then everything was going to be all right.

Ray tried to think on other things. Nixon was gone, though pardoned. The long, national nightmare that he'd been evading was finally over. So what? As far as Ray saw it, the country was still falling apart. "The end is near," he spoke to himself groggily. He then chuckled shortly, because he really didn't care. After all, the United States of America was really such a small and trivial thing to be concerned with, wasn't it? Ray yawned mightily as his thoughts began to drift and muddle. His burning eyelids refused to stay open.

Consumed by an exhaustion that had been building in him for months, Raymond fell to silent dreaming; though his silent dreams were filled with screaming terrors.

It was a new day. The sun had barely begun to rise. Thirty-seven year old William Cody, Nightfire's new sheriff as of two months ago, had not even been able to enjoy his ritual wake-up cup of coffee before Beth Green had called the station. Now he was standing in the house across the street from hers, staring at a dead old woman, who was laying in a pool of blood. "This is too much," he said with a shake of his head. Nightfire's small police force was busily trying to make sense of it all.

Janie Alberts had been a sweet, eighty year old woman. No enemies, as far as anyone knew. It just didn't make sense. "So, what've we got here, boys?"

"Murder, Sheriff."

"I can see that, Earl." The sheriff took off his big hat, set it on the table, and ran his hands over his thick, brown mustache. He then let out an irritated sigh. "What I meant was, how did it happen? Do we have anything to point our pistols at? Come on, Earl, wake up!"

The officer looked sheepishly away. "Sorry, Sheriff. Looks like somebody ripped out her throat." Earl's voice began to quiver. "Ripped it to shreds, I...I mean...she goes...went to my church, Sheriff. I'm not...doing too..."

"Aw, shit, Earl. Get outa here, boy. There ain't nothin' left for ya' ta do." Sheriff Cody patted his slowest officer on the shoulder and watched him leave the house. The man was clearly more of a mess than usual. This was not something that happened on a regular basis in Nightfire, Texas. Sheriff Cody shook his head. "Dirk? Beau? What's goin' on here? What are we lookin' at?"

Dirk stood from where he had kneeled by the body. He was visibly shaken, but he was also much stronger than most men on the force. "Well, Sir, it's like an animal did this. I mean, Earl was dead on. She's pretty badly...ripped open. There's no other word for it. And there's something else here too. I don't really like the impli..." Dirk was interrupted by the sound of someone slurping.

Both men turned to stare at Beau, who was drinking a steaming cup of coffee nonchalantly. "What?"

"Beau, what the hell are you doin'? We're standin' here with poor ol' Janie murdered on the floor, and you're drinkin' the coffee she left burnin' on the stove!"

"Actually, Sir, she didn't leave it. We made it when we came out here. None of us had time to get our coffee at the station. Sorry." He added as an afterthought, "Want some?"

"God damn it, Beau! Try to show a little respect here! This woman is dead, and your dirtyin' up her dishes like you own the place." The sheriff sighed again, then added, "Now get me a cupa that shit and let's get back to work here."

"Yes, Sir."

"Now what's all this you're sayin', Dirk? Somethin' else you said?"

"Yeah. Take a look. I think we've got ourselves a serious wacko." Dirk lifted something out of the old woman's hand with a pair of tweezers. It was a card of some sort.

"Who the hell is that supposed to be?"

Beau spoke from beside Sheriff Cody as he handed him a mug full of coffee. "Looks like Jonathan Frid to me."

"Jonathan Frid? Who the hell is that? Should I know him?"

"No," came Dirk's voice. "He's an actor. Don't you remember Barnabas Collins? The vampire character on *Dark Shadows* a few years back?"

"Oh yeah! Hell yeah. My wife used to watch that show all the time. Always made her want a bigger house." The implications suddenly dawned on him. "Shit! So we've got some sick bastard, wantin' us to think he's some sort of vampire, rippin' the throats outa helpless, old ladies. Shit on me!

"Well, we're gonna find out who did this if it's the last thing I do. Now that I'm sheriff, we'll be operating under a strict no tolerance policy. In other words, nobody gets away with shit! And there's only one thing I want this piece of shit murderin' psycho to have in common with Barnabas Collins. Cancellation." The sheriff took a sip of his coffee. "Damn! That is some good shit! What brand is that?"

"It's Folgers, Sir," Beau answered.

"Well shit. I guess I'll have to switch. This knocks the piss outa Maxwell House."

Morning changed quickly enough to noon, which, naturally and without great notice, changed to *after*noon. It was 4:45 by the time Bradley Stevens walked through the doors of Dan Parker's. Dan Parker's was a bar, grill, and arcade where Nightfire's denizens of all ages tended to accumulate. It was near the center of what passed for Downtown Nightfire. Bradley was seventeen years old, a junior at Nightfire High School. His shoulder length, brown hair hung loose and feathery, creating the perfect frame for his brandy-brown eyes and his glowing, white smile. He was just nearly six feet tall, and of course still growing. He wore a tight-fitting, long-sleeved shirt and blue denim bell bottom pants. He strode into the dining area of Dan Parker's as though he were at home.

"Just look at him!" Ann said to the other girls at her table. "He is so adorable! I swear, he looks so much like David Cassidy it's unreal! I'm so lucky he's all mine!"

"My ass he looks like David Cassidy! Nobody's that cute. Not in Nightfire anyway," Helen said.

Dori, who was one of the two older girls at the table, laughed at Helen. "Yeah. You're just mad that they took *The Partridge Family* off the air!"

"They're not totally off the air, Dori."

"Oh!" Ann said excitedly. "Do you watch that cartoon too?"

"Yeah!" Helen said, and the two girls broke into laughter.

Mati looked over to Dori. "Were we that silly when we were in high school?"

Dori grinned wickedly. "Not me."

Doris Gardener and Matilda Preston were both nineteen years old and enjoying their first year out of school. They had been best friends since the second grade, when Matilda had walked in on Doris French kissing Rubin Santana in the girls' restroom and vowed never to tell. It had eventually become the most innocent secret that the two girls had kept.

Annabelle Maryweather, while a year younger, had been their friend throughout high school. They had grown close through their involvement in the youth group at Nightfire United Methodist Church.

Helen Preston was the youngest of the four. She was only sixteen years old, but she looked much older. Senior guys were always asking her out, and Helen never complained. At the same time, however, Helen remained dissatisfied with the boys she dated. They were all just so immature.

Bradley's eyes searched the room until he found his prize: Ann. Bradley and Ann had been going out for a month now, and he was even beginning to think that he was in love. Of course, he had thought that several times in the past, but this time, he told himself, it was different. He walked over to the girls and pulled up a chair.

"Hey!" He grinned brightly. "What's up?" The girls all greeted him, and he took notice of Helen, eyeing the decorated bell bottom jeans and the bandanna in her hair. "So, Helen, you goin' for the Rhoda look or what?"

Helen wanted to be mad, but she just smiled. "Shut up, Bradley."

"I don't know. That theme song sort of fits you. Na na na na na na na na na..."

Ann reached over and grabbed his lanky hand. "Stop picking on Helen, Bradley. Pick on me instead."

"Hm. Maybe later. Grrrowl. You wanna go out tonight?"

"Sure, but where? What is there to do in Nightfire that we haven't done already a million times?"

"Well, there's always..."

"Don't *even* say Hilltop! Oh, gag! That place may be fine for you and the boys, but I think it's a total bore!"

Bradley seemed amused. "How 'bout a movie then?"

"There's nothing playing here that we haven't already seen! I'm holding out for *The Godfather, Part II* anyway."

"Well then how 'bout..." the goofiest grin that Ann had ever seen suddenly corrupted Bradley's beautiful face.

"What?" She asked.

"The Witch's Tree. Just you and me, babe ."

"Hm. That could be pretty groovy."

"Groovy my ass!" Helen interjected.

"Helen," her sister scolded, "stop talking about your ass. And don't curse in front of boys. It's an official girl secret that we even know how."

Bradley laughed and looked at disgruntled Helen. "What ass? Let's see it. You've got me all kinds of curious now."

Helen blushed, and Ann slapped Bradley playfully.

"What? I was just teasin'."

"You're always teasing Helen. I think you like her."

"Hm." Bradley took in the view of all the girls at the table. "I like all your friends, babe." He then made a little barking sound and bit the air in Helen's general direction.

"Stop!" Ann was trying not to laugh. "You can be such a goob sometimes! I swear! You're starting to sound just like Jeff!"

"*Goob*? Is that the best you can come up with? *Goob*? Oh! Oh, I'm so hurt!" He broke out into laughter.

Ann was getting a little bit irritated. "You're lucky you're so cute, Bradley Stevens!"

"Oh, no! It's Queen Beth!" Dori said under her breath. All of the teenagers turned to look in annoyance. Beth Green was always scolding them and calling their mothers to tell them what they did wrong and how they should keep a closer watch on their children. She honestly thought she was in charge of everyone's affairs. And she was the biggest gossip in town, which actually said a lot, considering that gossip was Nightfire's number one pastime.

"Did you hear?" Dori continued. "She found Janie Alberts murdered this morning! If the whole town didn't know what a freako Beth was she'd probably be a suspect herself!

She told Sheriff Cody that she noticed Janie didn't get the paper off her porch at the usual time, so she got worried on account of Janie's old age and all. Then, when Janie didn't answer the phone or the door, Beth found an unlocked window and crawled into the house."

"What a freak," Bradley said in disbelief. "And she's supposed to be a role model to all us hooligans." He considered. "I didn't know Janie Alberts."

"Well," Mati put in, "she went to Saint Paul, and she was pretty old. I don't think she did more than church. I think Ned probably knew her."

Bradley grinned. "Hell yeah, Ned knew her. In the Biblical sense, I'll bet. Ned's shaggin' all the old ladies in Nightfire! That old man's crazy!"

"Anyway," Dori continued, "she hovered around the murder scene all day and kept sending out reports via the gossip chain. Turns out somebody ripped Janie's throat out and put a picture of Barnabas Collins in her hand."

"Sick!" Bradley exclaimed. "Do they know who did it?"

"Nope. It could be anybody. And whoever it was is still at large."

Helen looked terrified. "Oh my god! What if he gets one of us? Oh, God! I hope they catch him before I go to bed tonight. I get so scared by stuff like this!"

"It's true," Mati said. "I took her to see *The Exorcist* last year, and I thought she'd never recover. She slept in my mom and dad's room for a month and a half."

"Oh, gosh!" Helen said. "Don't talk about that movie!" She covered her ears.

Bradley laughed. "Wouldn't it stink if Mati got possessed by Satan one night and went into Helen's room, and her head started spinnin' around, and..."

"Bradley! Stop it!" Ann scolded sincerely, "She really gets scared."

"Sorry." He looked at Helen. "Chicken."

"What is going on here?" All levity died with the sound of Beth's voice. "Bradley Stevens! What would your mother think! Young men do not frighten girls like that! That is entirely juvenile behavior! I just never!"

"Well," Dori spoke smartly, "maybe you should, Beth. It might knock that nail out of your..."

"Oh!" Beth wailed. "I have never been so insulted in my life! You just wait 'till your mother hears from me, Doris Gardener! You just wait!"

"I will, Beth. Don't sweat it. I'll probably smart off to her too, considering that I'm all grown up and all."

"Grown up my foot! Nineteen is not grown up, Doris! And you, most certainly, have some growing up left to do!" Beth stormed off, having finished whatever business she had at Dan Parker's, and she headed home to her precious telephone.

"Oh my gosh!" Bradley nearly wheezed, before he broke into uproarious laughter along with the rest of the table. "I can't believe you sometimes, Dori!"

"Well, she was asking for it. The bitch. She needs to mind her own damned business for once. What does that mean anyway: 'I never!'?" It's something only old ladies say. I swear! And she's not but five years older than your big broth...er." Dori thought better, all too late, about what she had just said. Everyone stared at Bradley expectantly. "I'm sorry, Bradley."

Bradley laughed it off, unnerved by the awkward silence. "Guys! Come on. So my brother died. I know. It was hard. But come on, it was four years ago! I'm cool. You can talk about him in my presence for God's sake. He was my brother. I *like* talking about him."

"Gosh," Mati ventured. "It seems so weird when you think about it. I mean, even though it's been four years. Donny just doesn't seem like someone who could...die. You know? I mean, we were in youth group with him. He was just so...alive!"

"I know," Dori said. "He was always the life of the party. He was so funny. Remember how much trouble he and Ray used to get into together?"

"Oh, I know!" The girls laughed, and Bradley tried to laugh with them, but all he wanted to do was hear them talk more. He missed his brother, and there was so much that he had missed out on. He had only been in Confirmation when his brother was a senior. He had never been in youth group with him like Dori and Mati. He loved to hear the stories they had. He loved to picture it in his head. He did remember all the trouble that Donny had gotten into with Ray though. He also remembered all the trouble that he himself had gotten into *because* of Donny and Ray. He sometimes wondered if it had contributed to his father's heart attack.

When Bradley thought about the deaths of his father and older brother, he felt so much older than he was. It was a lot to have been through in seventeen years. More than anyone else he knew of. But then, he knew he wasn't the only person in Nightfire to have lost a loved one in Vietnam. He wished his brother had run away with Ray and Lee when he'd had the chance.

Helen thought about Ray, now that he'd been mentioned. She had only been eleven when he'd left the country, but she remembered him fondly. Eleven year old boys are still into cars, bikes, and baseball, but eleven year old girls are always in love. Helen had suffered the most ferocious crush on Raymond Don. She sometimes wondered if that contributed to why she never got very serious with any of the boys she dated. No one was Ray. No one even came close.

"I miss Ray, too," Bradley spoke solemnly. "It was always like I had two older brothers, and not just one. You know?"

"Yeah," Mati said. "Wow. It's like, everybody's gone. It's just so weird. To think that they were here, and it seemed like the whole town belonged to them at times, and now, just like that, they're gone. They've been gone a while now, and they'll never be back."

Just then the door opened, and Jeffrey Mason burst in boisterously. "Woo-hoo! I knew I'd find you here! What's up, big BS?"

Bradley snickered without turning to face the senior football player. "I don't know," he muttered playfully to his female companions. "Should I respond to that?"

"It's your life," Ann said. She, however, was not at all amused.

Jeffrey came up to the table, sweat dripping down his long, black hair. Sweat causing the shirt he wore to cling to the sculpted muscles of his chest. He slapped the younger male on the shoulders, .You keepin' these bitches in line?"

"Shouldn't you be in practice or something?" Bradley turned his head slightly to see behind him and smirked at his sweaty friend.

"Shit. I don't know. Maybe so. So you wanna go hang out at Hilltop? Me an' the guys are gonna go up there an' puff the magic dragon, if you know what I mean." Jeffrey giggled mischievously.

"Nah, I'm gonna hang here for a while. Then I got a date with Ann. What the hell is wrong with you, man? You're sweatin' like a beast!"

Jeffrey laughed. "Yeah! Me an' a couple of the guys just beat the shit out of three niggers."

Bradley pulled away and turned his chair completely to face Jeffrey. "Jeff, man. That's not cool."

Jeffrey continued to laugh. "It was great! They were the three biggest niggers I've ever seen! And they took off blubbering like a bunch of fat-lipped babies! You should have seen it, Bradley! We were rolling!"

"So what did they do to you?"

"I don't know. Looked at us funny." He chuckled. "No, really. They started it. You know I'm not into all that racist shit, man. They started it, and we finished it! I swear!" He giggled some more.

Bradley shook his head. "And this guy's going away to seminary next year."

"You sure you don't wanna go to Hilltop, man?"

"Yeah. Say hi to everybody for me. You sure they're all gonna be there?"

"Of course they'll be there." Jeff shook his head as he walked away. "What else is there to do in Nightfire?" Jeff threw the doors wide open, as was his custom, and he almost ran into the man standing on the other side. As Jeffrey took off to join his friends at Hilltop, the man walked in, looking a bit perplexed.

"Who's this guy?" Mati asked.

"He looks new to town, if you ask me." Doris said, "And you know me. If I ain't seen him, he ain't from around here."

Helen rolled her eyes. "What a slut!"

Doris only laughed at this, as she continued to stare down the new guy. "Hm. He looks kind of pretty."

"Aren't you seeing somebody, Dori?" Bradley asked.

"Sure. Lots of 'em," she said with a sly grin and a wink. Bradley shook his head, but he could not repress his smile. "I leave no stone unturned. If you catch my meaning."

"I'll just pretend I didn't. And you keep your hands away from my stones, Doris."

Dori laughed, and she continued to watch the stranger. He seemed unsure what to do with himself. He was just sort of standing there, surveying the room. "I don't know. There is something familiar about him, now that I think on it. I can't place it, though. He looks like..." Doris studied him from the distance. She tried to place his fair complexion, his well groomed, shiny blonde hair, his large, blue eyes that seemed to sparkle even from across the room. It hit her suddenly, and a jolt of energy seemed to surge through her body, sending her instantly to her feet. "Ray!" Everyone turned to look. "Shit! Ray! Over here!"

The man suddenly lost his look of perplexity and replaced it with a glowing, white-toothed smile. "Doris? Doris Gardener?"

"You better believe it!" Doris ran to him now and flung her arms around him. He laughed and returned her sweet welcome.

He stood back. "Wow! You sure have grown up! How old are you now?"

"Nineteen." She spun around to show him every angle of herself. "And all grown up. We were just talking about you! Isn't that wild?"

The others at the table seemed not to have made up their minds that this man was in fact their Ray. When he lit up even more and began walking towards them, they made up their minds with great enthusiasm. They bombarded him with questions, wanting to know where he'd been, how long he'd been back, how long he was staying, everything.

Ray laughed at them. "Hold on, hold on! Let me figure this out first. He instantly grabbed Bradley and held him to his side. "You need no introductions, squirt. You look about the same, 'cept maybe a little bit girlier. What's with the hair? You goin' Hippie on me?"

"What about you?" Bradley pulled back and nudged Ray on the arm. "I couldn't tell who you were at first without the rest of it!" He reached up and mussed the other's shining hair.

"Hey! I got old." He grinned. "Actually, I just felt like a change a few years back. It's hot in Africa, man. Can't stand all that hair makin' it even worse."

"Africa? You went to Africa for all this time?"

Ray chuckled. "No, you little cum stain, I was all over the place."

Dori broke in. "'Cept Vietnam, right, my Artful Dodger?"

A haunted look passed over him, and just as quickly fled. "That's right. You don't blame me do you?"

"Honey, you just keep on lookin' like that, and I'll never blame you for anything."

"Oh please! You are such a tramp, Doris!" Helen all but shouted. She was on a very upsetting sort of mental roller-coaster at the moment, and she had no stomach for it. Ray Don had just walked through the doors of Dan Parker's for the first time in five years, looking as romance novel perfect as he ever had, and Doris was already shamelessly trying to sink her hooks into him. She knew it wasn't rational, but she felt a bit betrayed.

Ray glanced at the youngest girl without smiling, for only an instant, then he looked away and giggled. He saw Mati standing just beside the younger girl. He reached out and took her in his arms. "Mati, dear! You look astonishing!"

"Thanks," she said as she stood back by her sister and blushed. "You're not doin' too bad yourself. Do you still sing?"

"Ha! Not lately. I haven't really had the urge since..." He looked to Bradley, "...since I left," he lied quickly. He didn't want to bring up Donny's death right then. Not in front of Bradley. He was still unsure whether Bradley blamed him for what had happened. He wasn't even sure whether or not he blamed himself for it yet. Matters for another time. He looked at the young girl beside Mati. "Hi." He held out his hand. "Ray Don. Pleased to meet you."

Helen was horror struck! *He doesn't even remember me at all! He doesn't know who I am! I'm such an idiot!* She had no idea how to react. She wanted to throw up and feared that she would. *So stupid! How could I be so stupid!* She just stood there, staring at him.

Mati was quick to jump in and save her baby sister. She slapped Ray's hand away playfully and scoffed. "Don't play stupid, Ray! You know who this is!"

Ray looked at Mati quizzically. He really did not have any idea. "I...um..."

"Helen!" Mati said. "Don't you remember Helen?"

"Helen, Helen...uh..." He searched his brain for any Helen he had known in Nightfire, and his mind came up blank. "No." He looked very apologetically to Mati's hard gaze.

"My baby sister! Don't you remember my..."

"Oh!" Ray slapped his forehead, not knowing how he could have forgotten. "Your little sister! That's right! How could I forget! We used to laugh about how she wet her bed until she was in third grade!"

Oh, God!!! Helen wanted to scream! She could not remember ever having suffered through a more humiliating moment in her entire life! She wanted to pull out her hair and run out into the street screaming like a mad woman. Instead, dumbfounded, she just stood there stupidly, saying nothing, appearing to register nothing, looking to all the world around her like an absolute moron.

Ray whistled. "Wow, Helen. Wow. I would never have recognized you. You certainly have changed." He seemed to drift, staring at her. "For the better, of course."

Helen smiled. She didn't know how much more of this up and down roller-coaster she could take. She tried to avoid his stare, and her cheeks began to warm.

Ray went on, shaking his head and looking around at everybody. "I go away for a little while, and everybody gets..."

"Tits," Doris cut him off.

Bradley laughed out loud; once again charmed by Dori's blunt manor.

Ann rolled her eyes.

Ray looked over at the younger man, still standing at his side. "Yeah, you're right." He reached over and squeezed Bradley's left pec sensuously. "Hey, sailor. Buy me a drink?"

"Hands off my man, man!" Ann said.

Everyone laughed at this, and the chattering continued for a long while. The six of them sat down, and Ray bought everyone a Dr. Pepper and told them about the time he was in a camp that was attacked by lions. He told them about being thrown off of a ship and circled by a shark before Lee had managed to rescue him. He almost told them about being arrested in France, and how he had escaped. He stopped himself. He saw where his tales of adventure were going. If he told them about that, he would have to tell them *why* he had been arrested under false charges. He would have to tell them *why* he had been tossed off of a ship in the middle of the North Atlantic. He would have to tell them about Ireland and Rome.

"So why would someone just toss you off a boat like that, man? What did you do to tick him off?" Bradley asked innocently.

Ray's eyes shifted nervously. "Well...he thought I had something of his...employer's. But...I didn't." *That sounds good. Don't have to tell them that I had given it to Lee by then, or what it was.* "You know. Simple case of mistaken identity." He looked at his watch. "Well, I'd better get going; back to the hotel. I have some stuff to do before tomorrow." He stood up to leave. "But I'm here now. At least for two years." He laughed. "So I'll see y'all around."

Everyone said their farewells, and as Ray walked out, Bradley got up to follow him, leaving the girls to chat about the whole thing. "Hey!" He caught him at the door. "I'll walk you back to the hotel."

Ray smiled. "Good." The pair walked on.

***

"So, anyway," Ray said, "I stopped in to have a little chat with good ol' Sheriff Gilespe earlier today. Turns out he's moved on to other things."

Bradley considered the whole story of Sheriff Gilespe's nervous breakdown and subsequent commitment to the nut house for long term "rest." He laughed to himself. "Yeah. I guess that's one way to look at it."

Ray gave the younger man a puzzled sort of look, but then he went on as they walked. "So now it's Will Cody. I always thought he'd move to the top. So I said, 'Hey, Willy! I'm turning myself in! Let's talk about Ford.'

"Then he doesn't even get off the phone to ask me how I've been. Dirk tells me he's got his hands full with a murder. So the good Sheriff just waves me off, puts the phone down to his chin, says, 'Welcome home. You got forty-eight hours to get a job, or I'll shoot ya'.' Then he went back to his call. So I left and came here. I guess I'll go to the job placement office tomorrow morning and tell 'em my situation." Ray forced a smile.

Bradley just looked up at him. "I'm glad you're back, Ray. I've missed you."

"Yeah," Ray said. "I don't know. It's crazy. I went away and saw the big, wide open world, and still I managed to miss this place. In the dustiest corner of my heart, I really missed this messed up, little town. And everybody in it." He was silent for a moment, then, "So how's your family? Your mom, your siblings?"

"Mom's fine. Still worries too much. Brendan's always doing stupid shit. He's nine now. And Kate's gonna be seven tomorrow. She's already boy crazy." He thought for a moment. "You should go see Donny. We got him a real nice tombstone, you know? Right by Dad. We used some of the extra money Dad left us to put a nice, little bench out there. Just like Dad always said he wanted, so we could go and sit with him for a while when we visited."

Ray stopped walking, and Bradley followed suit. "Bradley," he weighed his words carefully, "I understand. You know. If you hate me for what happened to Donny." His eyes started to water. "If you...blame me. I couldn't *make* him leave. I couldn't do anything."

Bradley was touched on the deepest level by Ray's offering. His willingness to be a target for Donny's loved ones. "Ray," he put a hand on his friend's shoulder, "I don't blame you. None of us do. Not even Donny. He loved you right up to the end. I know that because they took his last letter home right off of his body. We got it about a week after we got him home. So we hadn't gotten it yet, when you called and we had to tell you what happened. But he talked about you in it. He talked about how much he missed talking to you, because he had so much to talk about, and he talked about how right you had been. How he should have gone with you, but he never would have known it had he not gone to Vietnam first. He quoted Rhett Butler. He said that if he got shot, that he would laugh at himself for being an idiot. And he said that Ray better laugh at him too. He said you were all that kept him going. Thoughts of getting home and laughing with you about the whole, terrible thing. Turning all of the horrors he'd seen into tasteless and irreverent jokes as only you could help him to do. He never once said a harsh word about you for doing what you felt was right. Not once in any of his letters." There was a pain in Bradley's heart, but it was a warm pain. He felt the ache of his missing brother, but it was mixed with the tugging on his heart by the joy at having Ray back.. Knowing that Ray was here to stay, at least for a while. No tears left Bradley's eyes though, for he had cried as much as he could during the last four years in mourning for his brother. He was too happy now. He had the next best thing to Donny, and his world seemed more complete than it had in a great, long while.

Ray wanted to sob. He wanted to let go of everything and just break down, weeping, and crumble into nothing on the ground.

Instead, just as the excruciating emotion threatened to push all of his tears through his eyes, he laughed. He laughed hard. Without warning, he grabbed hold of Bradley and hugged him as he laughed. "I loved your brother too." *And I love you*, he thought. *I'll be as devoted to you as I ever was to Donny*.

When the hug had ended, Bradley laughed. "So who all knows you're back?"

Ray shrugged, "Well, just you guys and the cops I guess."

"Didn't you even let your parents know you were back in the States?"

"Yeah right! I really want *them* to know. My mother who cries in shame whenever I'm mentioned. My father, the W.W. II vet from Hell. I really want him to drive his old ass down to Nightfire and beat me into the ground. No. I'm through with them. They moved away, when I was seventeen! I tried talking to them before I left. No. I've got nothing left to say."

"What about Tom?"

"Tom." Ray looked suddenly defeated. "No. I haven't talked to Tom. I'm pretty sure he'll hate me too."

"You don't know that, Ray. I think you're worried over nothing."

"Really? Why's that?"

"Tom was like a father to you! A *real* father, not your biological father. He never turned on you."

"But he thought I should have gone to Vietnam. He thought it was cowardly to run."

"But did he damn you for it? No. He let you disagree with him. He never tried to hold you back from making your own choices. He never tried to threaten you. He let you be a man. He let you choose. So what if he would have done things differently? You can't hide from him. He sees you as a son, you know? And he's gonna know you're back sooner or later. You're gonna have to face him. He was always good to you. He deserves that. Don't you think?"

"Yes." Ray looked to the sky and groaned. "Oh, God! I can't wait to have everything settled here! I can't wait to have all this stress off my back!" He smiled at Bradley, and he sighed. "All right. I'll go see old Tom. I'll go see him tomorrow. Does he still work over at *The Nightfire Chronicle*?"

"Yeah. And he's still living on the ranch."

"Good. Fine. Let's go to the hotel."

Bradley laughed at his friend's disposition. "Okay."

Just as the pair turned a corner, and the hotel was in sight, a scuffle caught their attention. A young Hispanic boy was yelling at a young black boy. Bradley moaned. "Oh, shit. The Santanas. Fuck."

Ray laughed. "The Santanas? You mean like that scrawny little prick Rubin? Looks like he's up to no good, same as always. "

"No." Bradley shook his head. "That's not Rubin. That's Herman."

"Ha! Herman! He looks just like his arrogant cousin!"

"I think you're gonna find that Rubin's changed. Well, physically. He's still arrogant. So are you. I think that's why y'all never got along. It does look like trouble though. It always is with them. They're always starting shit. Well, Rubin's not so bad anymore, and Juan actually tries to keep 'em all in line. It's just that little Herman creep!"

The two listened in on the heated debate. "I'm gonna cut you up, nigger! You better hand it over! I know you took it!"

"I didn't take shit, bro! Hold up! Why you pickin' on me?"

"'Cause you's the only nigger in the store, so who else is gonna run off with my wallet!" Herman, big for fifteen, but scrawny none the less, shoved the other teen up against the Santanas' green car and put a finger in his face. "Tell you what, Sambo. I'm gonna count to three, and you're gonna hand me the wallet. Or else I'm gonna kick your black ass all over the street!"

"Look, man! I don't want no trouble..."

"One." Breaking his word, Herman punched the other boy in the face with all his might. The black teen flailed his arms, obviously having avoided fights all his life. He tried to scramble away, but the stronger boy pulled him back and kneed him in the groin. Then he punched him again. "You wanna tell me you don't have it now, nigger? You want me to get Sheriff Cody on your ass?"

Bradley looked over to Ray, who was fuming. "So, what do you wanna do? I bet he'd love it if someone actually did call the cops."

"Who needs cops? That kid'll be road kill by the time they get here. We have to stop this now."

"Are you serious?"

Ray didn't answer. He just walked forward. Right into the middle of it.

"Oh, shit." Bradley followed him slowly.

"Hey! Santana! You wanna tell me what this is all about?"

Herman stopped beating the other boy long enough to try and put a name to Ray's face. He saw Bradley Stevens slowly easing up to Ray's side. "Who the fuck is this, Stevens?"

"This is Ray. Now answer his question. What's going on here?"

"None of your fucking business, gringo! This nigger took my wallet."

"Yeah right, kid!" Ray said with venom. "I think you just felt like messing with a nigger. I'm rememberin' the Alamo myself."

"Fuck you!" Herman slammed his fist into the black teen's face.

Ray was through with words. He ran to the teenagers and pushed Herman off of the other. "Get the hell out of here, Santana! And take your cocky cousin with you! I know you didn't drive here on your own, junior!"

Herman was furious! He lunged at Ray with his fist. Ray ducked and planted his own fist in the youth's slender belly, knocking the wind out of him.

The other boy slumped to the ground by the car, and Bradley went to him quickly and put a hand on his shoulder. "Hey, man. You okay?"

"I've been better," the other said.

Bradley looked up and saw that Ray had not finished with the other boy. "Oh, shit. Ray! Cool it!"

Ray was deaf to his friend's words. He saw only this young, stupid kid who had beaten a person for no reason other than the color of his skin. Herman was no longer even fighting back. Ray punched him again and again, and the boy fell over and held his face and his gut.

"Ray! Shit! You're a lot bigger than him! Stop it! Stop!"

The door of the drug store that they were all in front of opened, and Rubin Santana took in the sight of this man beating his little cousin to a pulp. He dropped his bag and just walked down the steps. Ray was kicking the young man on the ground with an endless rage. "Hey!"

Ray looked up. He was amazed. It was Rubin. He knew the face. And when he looked this hulking, muscular beast in the eyes, he saw that he was recognized as well. "Rubin?"

"Ray." Rubin looked down at his cousin, covered in blood and sobbing. He looked at Ray's fists, covered in blood. He looked over at Bradley and the other teen. He saw that the other was beaten up pretty badly as well. He saw blood on his cousin's fists, but none on Ray's face. He knew exactly what had happened. "Get the fuck away from him."

Suddenly Ray realized that he had spent all his rage. He had taught the kid a lesson. "Rubin, I..."

"I know, Ray. I told him not to go after the nigger." He pulled a wallet from his left hip pocket and held it up for all to see. "Dumbass left it on a shelf." He dropped the wallet, and it hit Herman's bloody face, causing the boy to squeal.

Ray suddenly felt his anger return. He snarled, and he kicked the boy again. Rubin made a monstrous face and grabbed Ray by the shirt. "Too far, Ray. When my little cousin acts up, I will handle it. Not you. I see what happened here, but next time you get *me*. No one puts the hurt on my family but my family!" He pushed Ray back slightly. Then, before Ray could even raise a hand to defend himself, Rubin slammed a powerful fist into his face. Ray stood dazed for a moment, and he felt like he was going to fall. Before he could decide whether or not he would manage to stay on his feet, Rubin's other hand met his chest and shoved him to the ground. Ray landed flat on his back, and the world seemed to spin.

Rubin collected his fallen cousin and shoved him into the car. He then glared at Bradley. "He should have stayed away. There's no room for him here. Not anymore. You best keep him out of trouble. If it can be done." Bradley and the other teen moved out of Rubin's way, as he got into the car and drove off, forgetting whatever it was he'd bought there on the steps.

"Holy shit!" Said the badly beaten stranger.

Bradley went to Ray. "Ray! Hey! You all right? Can you stand up?"

Ray put his hands to his face. "Man! That Mexican grew up big! I swear it! He was all long hair and muscles! Used to be such a little chump. Like his cousin."

Bradley helped Ray to sit up on the curb. He then looked to the other boy. He offered his hand. "Hi. I'm Bradley. Bradley Stevens. You must be new to town."

The other took his hand and shook it once firmly. "Sam. I'm Sam Turner. I was born here, but I lived most my life in Houston. Just moved back. Livin' with my granny. I sort of wish I'd stayed in Houston."

Bradley laughed. "Don't sweat it, Sam. It'll get better. Now you have friends." He nodded over to Ray. "That's Ray Don. He just came home himself. Ask around. He's a pain in the ass. Nothin' but trouble."

"That trouble saved my neck." Sam smiled and reached over to shake hands with Ray. "Thanks, brotha."

Ray took Sam's hand. "Sure. Any time."

Sam laughed at the three of them, sitting on the curb and nursing their wounds. Well, at least he and Ray were. Bradley was funny in another way, as he sat between them fretting.

Bradley stood suddenly. "Be right back." He took off running back to Dan Parker's. When he returned five minutes later, he was behind the wheel of his car. He leaned out the window. "Come on! Get in. Let's go for a drive!" Bradley knew that if he had said, *Let's go see my mom, so she can patch you up*, Ray, and probably Sam too, would not have come. As it was, the pair rose quietly and got in the car. Ray fell into the back and stretched out. Sam, quick to forget the beating, turned on the radio and tried to find a decent station.

"Mom! Hello?" Bradley walked through the door of his house and left it open for his friends. "Look what I brought home!"

Mrs. Stevens, Audri to her friends, rushed out of the kitchen, as she toweled off her hands. She hugged her young son and kissed him on the cheek. She then looked up and gasped. "Ray? Ray! Oh!" She went and hugged the young man ferociously. "Oh! What happened to your face! Oh! We'll have to fix you up! We can keep it from swelling too bad."

Just then Sam walked through the door. "Oh!" Mrs. Stevens said. "Is this a Negro? Did he do this to you?"

Bradley couldn't help but laugh, and neither could Ray. Audri Stevens was one of the most naive women on Earth, as far as either of them knew. And Ray was well traveled. "Yes," Bradley said. "This is a Negro. His name is Sam. And no, he did not do this. It was the Santanas that did this to both of them."

"Oh! Well what a horrible way to welcome you home, Ray! I don't like those Santanas. And they call themselves Christians. They go to church at Saint Paul every Sunday. Come into the kitchen. I'll get out the first aid box."

Ray knew that it was futile to argue with Mrs. Stevens. Bradley grinned triumphantly at the success of his trap.

When the three young men entered the kitchen, Mrs. Stevens had already taken some alcohol from the first aid box and was putting it on a rag. Ray's eyes went wide. "I really don't feel that bad, Mrs. Stevens. I...*Ouch*!" She put the rag to his face and started rubbing.

"Have to clean it out now, or it'll get infected, Ray. Oh, those horrible people! Picking on my delicate little Ray!"

"Delicate? I would have taken 'em if..."

"Yes, dear. I know." She patted his head and moved on to Sam. She repeated the process with a different rag. "Are you from Harlem?"

Sam looked at the woman as though she were crazy. "No. You?"

"Oh!" She laughed gleefully. "Goodness no! What a strange thing to ask! When I was a girl, there were lots of

Negros in Harlem though. My mother went there once, and she told me. I'm from Nightfire. That's where we are right now." She shook her head and laughed some more. "That is just so precious you asking me if I'm from Harlem. That's one for the diary! Of course, Africa's full of Negros too. You aren't..."

"No. I'm not from Africa. I was actually born here, raised in Houston. Now I'm back. Livin' with my granny." Sam could not stop smiling.

Bradley and Ray were both turning blue. Ray was lost in countless memories of ridiculous things Mrs. Stevens had said and done in the past. The pair of them were fighting so hard to keep in their laughter, and the struggle was not going their way.

"Oh, yes. Of course we have Negros here as well. Why, when I was in youth group at Nightfire UMC, we would have what we called Negro Fun Night."

Ray exploded, and Bradley followed. They laughed so hard that tears were streaming down their faces. "Mom!" Bradley got out between guffaws. "What are you talking about?"

Sam could no longer hold back his own laughter at this dingy white woman. Audri looked around at the three young men, and she was really quite puzzled as to what was so funny.

"Well, Negro Fun Night," she was interrupted by more extreme laughter from the boys. "Negro Fun Night was when we'd go pick up all the Negros and play games with them and sing songs."

Bradley was still laughing, and Ray was wheezing silently. "Mom! You're tripping! I swear!"

"Oh! Don't swear, Bradley." She looked down at her feet, to make sure that she wasn't tripping. "Oh. I'm all right, dear. The tile's been coming up there for years. I won't trip."

When the laughter finally died down, Mrs. Stevens served cookies and milk, and she joined the boys at the table. She caught up with Ray, and she realized that she knew Sam's mother from the days of Negro Fun Night. Finally, the boys got up to leave.

"Son, when you get home, I'd like you to take your brother out to a movie."

"Mom! I have a date."

"Oh! Well, I'm sure Ann wouldn't mind Brendan. He's a good boy. She's going to have to get used to little boys if she stays with you. Stevens men almost never have daughters."

"Mom!"

"Well, you've been going out for a month now. Don't you think she's planning to get married some day?"

"Mom! This is the '70's! People don't get married so fast..."

"Yes, Bradley. I know." She smiled, as though she were humoring him. "Now can't you take your brother? I think he needs some male attention. I found him wearing one of my nightgowns this morning when I woke him up for school. I tried to explain to him why little boys do not wear

Mommy's clothes, but he didn't understand. He needs you. You're his role model."

"Apparently not." Bradley rolled his eyes. Ray and Sam were laughing again. "I'll do something with him next week. Okay? But I can't take him out with me tonight. He'll ruin everything!"

"All right, Bradley." She seemed sad. "It's just hard for him. He never really had a father. Not for very long."

Bradley was irritated, but he knew it had been hard for his mom to raise sons by herself. "Okay. This week, Mom. I'll take him for a boys' night out this week. I promise."

She lit up. "Oh, that's so wonderful! He's going to be so excited! I'll tell him right away."

The three boys left the Stevens house and walked to Bradley's car. "Man," Ray said. "Your mom hasn't changed a bit. She's still this *Leave It to Beaver* Mombot from another world! I mean, who serves milk and cookies? Really?"

"I don't know," Sam said. "I think it's great."

"Yeah," Ray agreed. "Me too."

Bradley just shook his head. "So what are y'all doin' tonight?"

"Just gonna go to the hotel and brood," Ray answered. "You know, think about where I'm gonna live. Where I'm gonna work. That sort of thing."

"I got a date too, man," Sam said. "I met her in school on Monday. She showed me around n' shit. Name's Mary."

They piled into the car again. Same seats, only this time Ray sat up in the middle of the back instead of stretching out. Bradley turned on the ignition and drove. "The best place to go for alone time on a date," he advised, "is the Witch's Tree. Mary. Is that Mary Rhodes?"

"Yeah! She fine! And so sweet too."

Bradley smiled. "I tell ya', Sam. If I was gonna go interracial, I'd be all over that! Mary knows where the tree is. But don't go there tonight. That's where me an' Ann are going. There's another place though."

"Yeah?"

"The old Alexas mansion. It's been deserted forever! It's kind of creepy, but no one will bother you there. Take some candles or something and it's real romantic. Great place to talk. You know. It's real private. She'll know where that is too. It doesn't take too long to get the map of Nightfire down."

"Thanks, man. 'Preciate it."

"No problem, Sam. And we all usually hang out after school, either at Dan Parker's or at Hilltop. I'll show you around sometime. I'll make sure you're in with all the right people."

Ray contemplated the situation. It was amazing to him. Yesterday, they were three separate people, not at all a part of each other's lives. Now, it seemed they'd forged a bond, and would be together often. It was one of those groupings that just seemed to click.

He liked Samuel, and he no longer saw Bradley as anyone's "little brother." Bradley was a man all his own. He was someone that Ray could respect. An equal. Ray felt like he was home. It was so different from the way he'd left it, but it was still so much the same. Some things, he mused, would never change. The faces may change, the people may grow older, but Nightfire itself was constant as the sun.

Bradley parked the car at the side of the road. No one else was around. "That's it."

"It sure looks creepy tonight." Ann said. "I've never been here without a big group. It's scary. Have you ever seen her ghost?"

Bradley laughed. "No. Never. I think it's just an urban legend. Let's drive over to it."

"Why?"

"Scare all the ghosts off!" Bradley turned the car back on and floored it. He sped right toward the tree and stopped at the last possible second.

"Shit, Bradley! You could have killed us!"

"Yeah, but I didn't." He looked at the giant tree. It was quite a spectacle from a distance. The only tree in a giant field. Up close, it seemed safe. It was so open. He could see all around them. That was good, considering what had happened to Janie Alberts the night before. There was a killer on the loose in Nightfire. No way that killer was going to sneak up on him. Not by the Witch's Tree. He flashed his headlights and laughed about scaring the ghosts. Then he turned them off and looked at Ann.

"Aren't you scared?" She asked.

"Of what? The killer or the ghost?"

"The killer."

"Nah. Look around. He can't be hiding anywhere around here. Not even in the tree. It's bald. Then again, he could be really, really tiny."

Ann giggled. She enjoyed Bradley. She didn't love him. That she was sure of. He was just good for a fun time. She wanted to put him to the test. She wanted to see just how much fun he could be. "So what exactly did you have in mind for the evening?"

He shrugged. "I don't know. I thought we could talk. Maybe we could make out for a little while. Then I guess I'll take you home. I really just wanted to spend some time together. You know. Away from everybody else."

"We talk all the time though."

"Jesus, Ann. What would you like to do? I mean, you don't wanna go to the movies, you hate Hilltop, you don't like to talk. We can't just make out you know. If we don't do other things, we don't have much of a relationship."

"But that's just it! I want to do other things with you, Bradley! You're too nice! You never even grab my tits!"

Bradley was floored. "You...you want me to grab your...tits? Is that what this is all about?" He was thankful for the dark of night. He hoped she couldn't see how he was blushing.

"More, Bradley. I want you." She reached down and unbuckled his belt, "All of you."

Bradley pulled away from her. "Ann...I...I can't."

"Why not?" She leaned over and kissed him. Then she crawled over the seats and spoke from behind him. "Don't you like me?" She giggled seductively, and she tossed her blouse up front.

Bradley was shaking. He wouldn't turn his head to look at her. "Ann, I just...I want there to be more to our relationship. That's all." Her jeans flew into the front seat. Bradley closed his eyes and swallowed hard. He was sweating, and he thought that he would surely throw up. "I mean...I just..." Her bra landed on his head. He pulled it off and piled it on top of her other clothes.

"Turn around, Bradley. Turn around and look at me."

"No."

"Bradley!" Ann laughed at him. "Why not? Are you scared or something?"

Bradley held his breath for a moment. "Yes," he said at last. "I'm petrified. I've never...done that before. I don't know if I'd be any good at it. And what if...what if something...happened. You know?"

Ann laughed affectionately, and she put her hand on Bradley's quivering shoulder. "Don't worry, Bradley. I won't get knocked up or anything. It's the wrong time of the month. I promise. And I'm sure you'll be great at it. Because you're a great kisser. Now turn around."

"All right. All right." He turned his head slowly, and he forgot his fear at the sight of her. His body was suddenly on fire. All he felt was yearning for her.

"So are you gonna join me back here? Or do I have to put all my clothes back on so we can talk all night?"

"Just let me turn on the radio. It's kind of creepy with the silence and all."

The radio came on, and Bradley crawled into the back seat. His own clothes were quickly piled on top of hers in the front. As they took their relationship to the next level, Bradley found the song on the radio amusing. It was trying to relate a romance to Napoleon's surrender at the battle of Waterloo. Bradley almost laughed. *That's me*, he thought, *I didn't have a chance.*

When it was over, he held her and told her how much he loved her.

Samuel Turner crawled through the window of the old Alexas mansion. He turned on the flashlight and looked around. "Wow," he said. "They didn't even take the furniture when they left."

Mary Rhodes crawled in after him. "I know. And nobody wants to rob the place either. People say it's haunted pretty badly."

"That's what you said about that tree that Bradley went to. Ain't there no place in this town that ain't haunted?"

Mary laughed. "Live here long enough, and you'll begin to wonder."

"So why didn't we come here earlier?"

"Because you were off gallivanting and getting your face beat in earlier."

He laughed at himself. "Yeah. Ain't gonna do that again."

"Good," she said, "because you have the cutest face." She grabbed his flashlight and turned it off. She kissed him gently on the lips.

"I may come to like this town after all," Samuel conceded.

Suddenly the pair heard a door creak upstairs. "Shit!" they both breathed out. There was the muffled sound of something making its way quickly across the floor and to the stairs.

"Go!" Samuel said. "Let's get out of here!" Mary launched herself out the window, and she waited for Sam to follow. The sound had gotten to the stairs. Someone was walking very fast. *The ghost.* Samuel was horrified. He listened to the footsteps descending the stairs, and he heard a low growl. "Oh, shit! Shit!" He tried to get out the window, but the footsteps had gotten faster, the growl had become something closer to a roar. "It's a fuckin' demon! Fuck! Run! Run!"

Mary was screaming, and she was crying as she did just that. She could hear Sam screaming, and she could hear the demon snarling. She did not dare look back.

Sam felt the weight of the monster knock him to the floor. He felt its hot breath on his neck, as warm saliva gently dripped down from its fangs. He knew it had fangs. It had to. It was something right out of Hell. A demon. Samuel wept silently in that instant. He thought about Mary telling him that the woman who'd been killed had been torn apart, as if by a wild animal. Samuel lost control of his bladder at the instant the monster's cold snout finally connected with the flesh of his neck, and he knew that he was going to die.

CHAPTER 2
THE MYSTERIOUS VALEN ALEXAS

Samuel heard the sound of the monster's moist jaws snapping open, and he prepared for the end. But there came a sudden and chilling interruption. "Raksha! Come."

The pressure left Sam's back, as the demon took its leave of him. The fierce jaws that Sam had imagined never tore into his flesh. Yet Sam felt no relief. There was someone else in the house; someone commanding this monster; this monster who would have torn him apart, just as Janie Alberts had been torn apart at the throat by some mysterious murderer. Sam could only imagine that the monster had been called away by someone so much fiercer. He kept his eyes shut, hoping the pair would leave him; hoping that they would ignore him till sunrise; for surely such terrible things could not endure the light of day.

The lights came on, flooding the room and assaulting Sam's clenched eyes. He opened them.

"Please, forgive Raksha. She was just doing her job, and she has her ways. You're safe now, though. I won't let her harm you." The voice fell to gentle laughter. "It's all right, sir. You can look at me. I won't bite."

Samuel slowly rose from the floor. He sat up, shaking, and he turned to face this voice. To his total astonishment, this voice was not produced by some monster. The man looked not to be threatening in the least; and the demon, as the light now revealed, was actually a wolf. A wolf that looked friendly and content, as she panted at her master's side. "You gonna kill me?"

The man laughed soothingly. "No."

"They told me this place was deserted."

"It was." The man smiled, then he looked at Samuel's soiled clothes. "Hm. I like the way you dress. I apologize for the mess that Raksha made of you. Please won't you stand?"

Samuel did, slowly, and his eyes shifted quickly from side to side, looking for an escape.

"Ah, yes! You look to be about my size. I think you'll be fond of my wardrobe. Most of my better clothes haven't been sent yet, but my suitcase is full of beautiful things. Not quite like the garments you're wearing now, but still quite fine. I can't have you leaving such a mess."

The boy looked confused. "This is your house?"

"Yes. I'm Valen Alexas. This house has been in my family for years, but I have lived abroad. Let's go upstairs now and get you some clothes to wear. And perhaps you can explain to me why you have broken into my house."

It was afternoon at last, though it seemed as though a week had passed since morning to Sheriff William Cody. The sheriff was a strong man, and he was very much a man of the people. He had come to know and love practically every family in town; all races. He was very passionate about true justice. In his mind, true justice and prejudice of any kind could not exist in the same time or place.

Still, Sheriff Cody was no saint. He was one of Nightfire's Good Ol' Boys first and foremost. He loved to talk and "shoot the shit" with any man who'd listen. He tried to watch his mouth around women. He didn't think they would appreciate all of the things he liked to say about this person or that. It wasn't that he thought they were less intelligent; rather, he thought that they were more high class than himself, and his own wife Angelina was the finest of them all. She could be a crazy lunatic at times, but she was a fine woman just the same. It was one of her lunatic ideas, in fact, that had brought Sheriff Cody here today, after a second murdered body had been found.

The door to the little, silver trailer home opened, and the fifty-two year old woman who stood behind it greeted the sheriff with a decidedly predatory grin. "Sheriff Cody. I've been expecting you."

The sheriff huffed. "Am I supposed to be impressed by your eerie psychic powers now?"

"Ha. No. Angelina called me. She told me you might be difficult. Please," she gestured with her arm, "come inside."

The boys on the force better not find out about this. Me with Mary the witch, after all my bluster. The sheriff entered Mary Jean Donovan's little home, and she seated him at a round table with a red cloth covering it.

"So what? Are you gonna tell my fortune?"

She shrugged, as she sat down opposite him. "If that's what you really want. However, I do not think that it is." She looked into his soothing, gray eyes, "You are in pain. You are in fear."

"Damnit! How much did Angelina tell you?"

"She told me that you were coming; that you might be difficult. But then you knocked on the door, and I had to let her go. You're uncomfortable with this. With me. Sheriff Gilespe often..."

"I know! But I'm not him. I never liked it that he came to you like he did. That he seemed to rely on you. All your supposed psychic power wasn't enough in the end, after all. He's still been locked up in the bug house, and they've thrown away the key! I don't want to end up like that. I won't!" He sighed. "I don't give you any credit. I think you're either a fraud or a crack pot. I'm only here because Angelina insisted that you could help me. That you could point me in the right direction. So I thought I'd give you a chance." He leaned in. "However, if you're *too* accurate, I'll have to be suspicious of it. I don't fall fer all that psychic shit the way my wife does."

Mary Jean smiled. "Of course. You're a practical man. I can see that. You won't end up like your predecessor. No. You will do well for yourself. But you have other concerns. Something that you are afraid of. Something that is assaulting you. Please, talk to me. If you will not accept me as a psychic, at least accept me as a councilor. I have never left anyone unsatisfied. If I were never on target, the townspeople wouldn't talk about me as they do. They wouldn't come to me again and again. They wouldn't call me Mary the Witch."

The sheriff thought it over. What did he have to lose? He could not remember anything like this ever happening in Nightfire, and he was at a loss as to how he should find the murderer. He was unsure where to start. "Well, okay. There's been two murders in the past two days. Well...nights. We just never find 'em till morning. Yesterday, we found Janie Alberts. Today it was a young Negro boy. A stranger. I never seen 'im before. We're still tryin' to figure out who he is. Where he came from. I don't know. But it don't matter fer shit that I don't know him. That's two murders. Two murders that happened right under my nose. Grisly murders. And I don't have any suspects. That's where my wife was tellin' me you'd be of some help."

"Yes." Mary Jean seemed strangely distant. She seemed to be looking at things that weren't there. "There is a monster in Nightfire. A terrible person. A man."

"That's no big insight. How many female serial killers you ever heard of?"

"Point taken, Sheriff. I will try to see some more. Hm. I learned something the other night. There were omens. A vampire has taken residence in Nightfire. But it is not this vampire for whom you should be looking."

The sheriff seemed stunned. He was. The body had been found that morning at the Johnson Ranch by Tom Johnson himself. Sheriff Cody knew that the details of the first murder had already spread across town, but the details of this one had been kept more or less under wraps. For one, the victim was someone that no one knew; and second, Tom Johnson knew how to keep his mouth shut. Few people would even know that there had been a second murder until the paper came out the next day. The vampire connection: that's what had frightened Sheriff Cody. "Why do you say that?"

"Why does it matter that I have said this? I am telling you that finding the vampire is not your biggest problem."

"My white ass it ain't! Both bodies were found in a similar state. They were torn apart at the throat. And there was a picture in their hands. It was some damned TV vampire in Janie's, and the Negro boy had a picture of Bella Lugosi. Count Dracula himself! There is some sick bastard out there wantin' us to believe in vampires. Now I'm just itchin' to know how the hell you know about it!"

"It is my gift. I know that you don't suspect me of anything in this case. You know deep down that I have had nothing to do with it. You have a great instinct about people. Almost a sixth sense. You are gifted in your field."

The sheriff wanted to argue, but he could not. He just didn't believe that Mary Jean could be involved in the murders. He felt it in his gut. Maybe she was a good guesser. Maybe someone had managed to tip her off. Maybe Angelina had said more than the witch was letting on. "All right," he conceded. "Maybe you're right about that, Mary Jean. But just the same, why don't you go ahead and tell me everything you know."

Mary Jean offered him a smug and toothy grin. "Very well, Sheriff Cody. Let me tell you the rest. There was wolf's hair on the wind..."

The sheriff's heart skipped a beat. "We found wolf's hair at the scene of the crime this morning. Then I sent some boys out to Janie's place, and they found it there as well. You have my attention, Mary Jean."

She nodded. "This is a clever fiend, but not *so* clever. He is clever in his stealth alone. Otherwise, he is a clumsy fool. He is a stranger here. He is a pawn. You will not find him if you look for this vampire." She closed her eyes and seemed to strain. "The vampire is going to win." She opened her eyes and looked to the sheriff solemnly. "And there is absolutely nothing that you can do to stop it."

Ray Don was sitting on the side of his bed in the dim light of his hotel room. His mind was in chaos. The Gideon's Bible on the night stand seemed to be taunting him, laughing at him. He wanted to tear it to shreds and throw whatever remained out into the street to be run over again and again by the passing traffic. He needed a diversion. He needed a way to get the evil book off of his mind. He focused on the little torn off corner of notebook paper just beside the Bible. Ray didn't know what to do. He wanted comfort in the worst way, but he was having a difficult time trying to differentiate between right and wrong. He didn't believe in God, and this was a relatively new development. It was now Ray's word that determined right and wrong, and every moral dilemma seemed to be too much.

Late that morning, Doris Gardner had come by. Ray, having slept in, crawled out of bed and answered the door in nothing but his boxer shorts. Doris had not been the slightest bit embarrassed by this. She had smiled mischievously and walked right in. By the way she had flirted and the continuous stream of sexual innuendoes, Ray had known what she had wanted from him easily. The problem was that he wasn't sure it was right. He really didn't know her that well anymore. Not the woman she'd become. It was hard for Ray to think of Doris Gardner as anything but a fourteen-year-old, giggling child. Ray had clumsily explained to Doris that he was very tired, and that he would probably see her later on, but he needed to sleep.

Not in the least bit discouraged, Dori had written her number on the corner of a sheet of notebook paper and torn it off for him, so that he could call her when he had more energy.

What's my problem? He thought to himself now, as he reached over and brought the paper closer to his eyes. *If there is no God, then all things are permitted. But does that make them right?* Ray wanted to cry. He was so confused, just as he had been ever since he and Lee had stumbled upon that...

There was a knock at the door. "Come in!" Ray decided that it didn't matter to him who walked in at all. He needed a distraction, and he needed it now.

"Hey, Ray!" came the more than welcome voice of Bradley Stevens. He started to laugh. "Guess what happened to Sam!" The teenager laughed some more. "He has got the dumbest luck!"

Ray smiled, so relieved by the interruption, and he saw Sam walk in behind Bradley and close the door behind him. "What happened?"

"Tell him!" Bradley said to Sam.

"Well..."

"Gosh, Ray!" Bradley interrupted the other teenager. "Do you not believe in light?" He flicked a switch on the wall and activated the ceiling lamp, illuminating the entire room.

Ray squinted against the brightness. "That's the real question, isn't it?"

"Go on!" Bradley said. "Tell him."

"Okay," Sam said. "It's not that big a deal, really. Bradley just thinks it's too funny..."

"He got busted at the old Alexas mansion last night!" Bradley blurted out.

"Busted?" Ray asked. "Who the hell would care whether or not you were trespassing at that creepy, old place?"

Sam gave Ray an amused look. "The owner."

"The owner? You mean somebody lives there?"

"Yeah. He said the mansion'd been in his family for years, but he been gone for a while. Now he back."

"From where? Who is this guy? That mansion's been abandoned since before I was born! Way before I was born!"

"Said his name was Valen. He was actually pretty nice. He let me clean up and give me some new clothes after his pet wolf scared the piss out of me."

"Pet wolf?" Ray was getting excited. There were strange things afoot. Distracting things. "Didn't they say that Janie Alberts looked like she'd been attacked by a wild animal? Did this guy just get into town?"

Sam seemed hesitant to answer. "Yes, and yes. He just got in yesterday morning at about two AM. But you ain't thinkin' that..."

"Why not?" Ray asked as he stood excitedly. "He got here just in time to let his wolf rip Janie apart. Then, maybe he put that picture in her hand, because he's a sick fuck who wants everyone to think some vampire did it! It makes perfect sense!"

"Yeah, but ain't that about the same time you got here too?"

Ray shrugged. "Well, yeah. But I don't have any wild animals to help me tear people's throats out. Let's go!"

Bradley was lost. "Go where?"

"The Alexas mansion! We'll pay our new neighbor a visit. Ask 'im if he's killed any old ladies lately."

"You serious?" Sam asked. "Man, he ain't that bad! It has to be some sort of coincidence. He was a real cool guy."

"Yeah, yeah. That don't mean shit." Ray said, as he threw on his shoes and headed for the door. "You're driving, Bradley."

"Of course I am. I'm the only one who has a car."

The two teenagers just looked at Ray as though he had lost his mind. "Come on," he said with a grin. "It'll be fun."

"Fun?" Bradley asked. "What if this guy *is* the 'Vampire Killer,' as christened by *The Nightfire Chronicle*? How much fun are we gonna have then?"

"Lighten up, Stevens." Ray shrugged and then laughed. "If this guy is the Vampire Killer, then he'll probably be sleeping anyway. Right? Right. So let's go."

Ray headed out the door, and his two young friends followed helplessly. Bradley remembered the words of Rubin Santana the day before on the matter of Ray returning to Nightfire. *'You best keep him out of trouble. If it can be done.'* Bradley considered that. *No,* he concluded, *I don't suppose that anyone can keep Ray out of trouble. That would be just about as futile as cramming God into a jelly jar.*

The trio arrived at the old Alexas mansion in little time. Ray bolted out of the back seat as soon as Sam pulled the seat forward, and he walked quickly to the front door. Sam and Bradley followed. "Where is this guy's car?" Ray asked.

"He don't have no car." Sam answered. "He ain't got all his stuff here yet."

"Interesting," Ray said.

Bradley stepped up onto the great front porch of the mansion. He studied it. As he looked around, he spoke quietly. "Well, if I were a vampire, this is where I'd stay. It's the perfect place. In fact, I don't think I've ever even seen this house in the light of day until now. And you can't even see any other houses from here. Just trees and grass, and dirt road. Very isolated."

"No shit." Ray said. "It's also the perfect place for a serial killer and his evil pet wolf."

"Raksha ain't evil, man. She jus'..." Sam stopped cold. He heard that familiar, low growl. "Oh, shit."

"Where is that coming from?" Ray looked around. "I'm knocking."

As Ray knocked on the door, Sam and Bradley both backed away slowly, as though the door were going to explode. Sam was embarrassed that Ray would be so out to get the man who had treated him so well the night before. Bradley was just scared. He had no desire whatsoever to meet a sadistic serial killer face to face.

Ray's knocking was answered by a ferocious snarling. Ray backed away from the door, and the wolf appeared at the window; all teeth and drool. It was a horrifying image to behold. All three men gasped and backed further away. Bradley and Sam backed completely off of the porch. The wolf continued to growl threateningly.

"Ain't nobody home, Ray! Don't fuck with the guard dog, man!" Sam warned.

"Let's just give him a minute. It's a big house. Maybe it takes him a while to crawl out of his coffin in broad daylight." Ray smirked at the wolf in the window, and he marched back up to the door. He started to bang on it with his fist, as he shouted, "Hey, Dracula! Wake the fuck up!"

The wolf began to go ballistic. Bradley didn't want to hang around and wait for the man to open the door, especially after Ray's taunting comments. "Come on, Ray. He's obviously not home, and you're gonna give that animal a stroke."

"Yeah," Ray agreed. "I guess you're right. We'll come back later then. I have to go down to the employment office anyway." Ray looked at the wolf as he began to walk away. He made an angry, toothy face and growled mockingly at the snarling beast. He then laughed and turned away. "Okay, let's go."

Just then, Ray heard the sound of glass shattering behind him, and Bradley and Sam's eyes went wide with horror as they turned and bolted to the car. Ray turned around to see the wolf on the porch, shaking the glass of the window from its fur. "Oh, shit."

Ray leapt from the porch and tried to run to the car, but the wolf was on top of him in no time, tearing at his pants with its deadly jaws, growling at Ray with immeasurable rage.

"Oh, fuck! It's gonna eat him!" Bradley didn't know what to do.

Sam considered the previous day, when Ray had come between him and Herman Santana. Sam could not turn from the opportunity to repay the debt. He may have been scrawny, but he was no coward.

The monster latched on to Ray's back pocket, as the young man tried to crawl to the car. "Guys. I'm in a bit of distress here." Ray could not stop thinking that the wolf would lose its grip at any moment and try to get a meatier hold on him.

"Raksha," Sam said. The wolf stopped growling and regarded him. Shakily, Sam eased over to the wolf and knelt down beside it. He reached out. "It's okay, girl." And he patted the creature gently on the head. "Ray's with me. Please let him go. He's just an ass hole. He don't know when to stop playing."

The beast huffed. Then it grudgingly released its prey and began to lick Sam's hands.

Sam laughed. "You better get in the car now, Ray."

"Right. Thanks." Ray wasted no time. When he was safely in the car, along with Bradley, Samuel patted the wolf again on the head and joined them. The three drove off and breathed a collective sigh of relief.

"Well," Ray ventured, "I'd say we now have candidate number one. This Valen Alexas and his evil pet wolf. How the hell did you do that, Sam?"

"I don't know. I just took a chance. She and I were on good terms last night, after Valen introduced us. And she seems really, really smart. Unnaturally smart. I just thought that maybe I could vouch for you."

"Good thing it worked, or we'd both be dog food."

"Hoo! Thank God." Sam was letting the stress of the moment catch up with him, and he was shaking uncontrollably. "Me and Mary are definitely not going to let Bradley recommend any great date spots in the future. That's for sure."

"Hey," Bradley spoke from the driver's side, "How was I supposed to know that some guy and a man eating wolf had just moved in?"

"Well how was your date, Bradley?" Ray asked.

Bradley hesitated, but he couldn't help but smile stupidly. "Oh, it was okay. You know. We had a good time."

"What did y'all do?"

"Uh... nothing. You know. We ... uh… talked... and... uh... stuff."

"Gee...uh...Bradley," Ray said mockingly. "Uh...I don't suppose you could be...uh...leaving anything out."

Bradley laughed. "Shut up, Ray. We had a good time. But I didn't see her today. She wasn't in school. I've gotta call her when I get home, but first I need to get Kate a present for her birthday party today."

"Yeah, you better call her," Ray scolded. "Especially after...uh..."

Sam and Ray both laughed at Bradley, and Bradley turned bright red, still unable to repress his goofy smile.

Early that evening, Ray crept into the offices of *The Nightfire Chronicle*, the newspaper that had been servicing Nightfire,

Texas since the town's foundation in 1847. Ray found his way to the chief editor's office. Thomas Johnson was seated at his desk, smoking a pipe and reading over something on blue paper.

"Hey, Old Tom. What'cha know?"

The man looked up from his paper and put it on the desk, astonished. "Ray!" He stood up, not believing his eyes. "I'd heard rumors, but I swear I didn't believe them." He went over to the young man and hugged him fiercely. He then stepped back and looked the young man over. "You cut your hair, and you got taller. You look good, kid. A sight for sore eyes. Why didn't you come sooner?"

Ray shrugged. "I thought you would be pissed at me for what I did."

"What? You mean that whole draft-dodging thing?"

"Well, yeah. You told me that you didn't agree. You said I should have gone."

"Ray, don't you know me better than that? I didn't agree, and you heard me out. Then you did what you damn well pleased. You did what you damn well thought was right. I respected you for that. Even before I changed my mind. No matter, son. It's all in the past. And the past grows ever more distant."

Ray was surprised. "You changed your mind?"

"Well yeah! That's my prerogative ain't it?"

"Why?"

"Well, Ray, I could only help to bury so many kids who died for nothing. You know. We didn't have any business bein' over there. You said so yourself. And you were right.

But I was never cross at you for leaving, even before. You can ask anyone. I would light a candle for you at Saint Paul every week. I loved you. You were like the son I never had."

Ray started to cry, and he covered his eyes in embarrassment.

"Hey, now. Don't fight that. What're they for?"

Ray removed his hand and let his tears show. "For relief, for regret, for guilt at my lack of regret, for...thankfulness. I'm so happy that I still have you, Tom."

"Ray, you'll have me as long as I breathe. I'm so glad you're back. How long are you staying?"

Ray laughed, as his tears began to fade. "Two years. Maybe longer. Depends on how things go. But even if I leave in two years, I've got the freedom to come back now whenever I want."

"Good. So where are you workin'?"

Ray rolled his eyes. "Oh, God! There's a tale. I went down to the employment office today, and I told 'em my situation. Turns out the old bat at the desk hates draft-dodgers. Her nephew was killed in the conflict. I told her it wasn't my fault, because she seemed to be blaming me. Then I told her that if he had done like me he wouldn't have died for the damned stupid government. So then she just glares at me, and I'm like, great, Ray, you've done it again. Then she asks me what kind of public service work I was looking for. I told her just anything, as long as I don't have to work with kids, old people, or retards."

Tom started to chuckle heartily.

"You see where this is going, don't you? You know her, right?"

"Ray, I know everybody in Nightfire. And Gretta goes to my church. She and that very special son of hers never miss a service."

"I don't know how I do it, Tom. I just have a gift for pissing people off. So she tells me about her son and all his problems with Downs Syndrome and how wonderful children are in general, and I'm like, yeah, yeah, so just find me some nice job painting signs or something. Then she looks through her books and says, 'Well, Mr. Don. It appears that the only opening we have is at the recreation center, working with children and young teens.' And I'm like, well, why don't you look a little bit harder, lady, and she's all, 'You can start Monday, Mr. Don. Or perhaps you'd prefer it in jail.' So I took the job, and she's all smug. I know she just did it to spite me. I don't wanna work with kids. They're just so...slimy."

Tom chuckled some more. "Ray, you haven't changed a bit. You're still an ass. I think Gretta probably did you a great favor. Come 1976, you'll be bawling your eyes out if you have to leave those kids."

"Bull shit."

"Correct me if I 'm wrong now, son, but, didn't you almost burn that rec center down when you were eight?"

Ray rolled his eyes again at the revelation he feared Tom was getting to. "Yes, I did, but it was an accident! I was just a kid! Tell me Old Man Morris isn't still alive and..."

Tom was loving it. "Oh yes, he's alive and well. Still running the rec center. Still talks about you when he gets drunk. You're in for quite a ride come Monday morning, boy. Oh, yes! He remembers you well."

"Great. I don't suppose I can still just go to jail. It might be easier."

"Oh, stop whining, Ray. You'll do okay. You always do. It's only two years. Then you can come and work for me, if you want; here, or at the ranch, or do whatever you want, man. Your debts will be paid. You'll be free again."

"Ah, whatever. I'm sure you're right. I'll deal with it. Assuming the kids don't piss and shit me to death. So how's Abi?"

"She's fine. Still teaches Sunday school every week. You should come by tonight. Hell, let's go right now. I'll put somethin' on the grill. Abi'll be thrilled to see you!"

Ray smiled. "All right, Tom. That sounds like just the medicine. It's so good to be home."

"Yes," Tom nodded. "It's good to have you home, Ray. Just try not to get into too much trouble over the next two years. Okay?"

Ray looked demoralized. "Who? Me?"

Thomas Johnson only laughed, and the pair walked out together.

Bradley got home at just after five. He entered as quietly as he could, carrying the little, brightly-wrapped package under his arm. His mother startled him by suddenly appearing in the entryway. She whispered, "Bradley, where have you been?"

"Sorry, Mom. I couldn't find Sweet Sixteen Barbie anywhere. I looked all over."

"Oh, no! What did you get instead?"

"The lady at the store said that Sun Valley Barbie was the next best thing, and she had one left. So I got her that. Do you think she'll like it?"

"Oh, I'm sure she will. When you take off Barbie's clothes, they all look alike anyway."

Bradley's nine year old brother Brendan came into view then, fully dolled up with lipstick and rouge. "Look, Momma. I'm a girl!"

"Oh! Brendan! Go wash up right now! You're going to attract the wrong kind of attention."

"It was Kate's idea!"

"Brendan, go on now!"

"Fine!" The young boy stomped off in disappointment.

Audri whispered pleadingly to her older son, "Boys' night out!"

Bradley rolled his eyes and nodded his head. "Tomorrow, Mom. I promise."

"Bradley!" Little Katelynn Michelle ran into the dark entryway and wrapped herself around her big brother's leg.

He patted her head. "Happy birthday, Grover ."

She backed away and put her hands on her hips. "I'm not Grover today! I'm Kate, because it's my birthday. Mom says that I only get presents if I don't talk like anything off *Sesame Street*."

"Tell you what; you get one from me anyway."

"See, Mom! I told you God was on my side!"

Mrs. Stevens put a hand to her head in exasperation. "Oh, Kate, go on back to your guests. Now that your brother's here, it's time for cake."

"Yes!" She made a triumphant gesture with her fist.

"Here you go, Stink." Bradley handed her the package. "But don't open it until after you blow out the candles."

"Okay!" She snatched it from his hands. "Let's go!" She ran off back to the party and shouted, "Happy birthday to me! Now! Start singing!" A moment of silence passed. "Sing it now, Goddamnit!"

"I'll go get the matches, dear." Mrs. Stevens looked as though she were about to break down. "I don't want to scold her at her own birthday party, Bradley. I don't know where she picks it up! She can be so...strong willed! Please say something to her nicely. She looks up to you. I don't want the other girls' mother's to think we have a broken home. I don't want them to think she learns her bad language from me! I just...birthdays can be so hard for me."

"It's okay, Mom. I'll get her to stop."

"Thank you, Bradley."

From the other room, they heard four year old Eleanor Jones from next door giggling loudly before shouting, "Goddamnit!"

Mrs. Stevens gasped.

"Don't worry, Mom. I'll take care of it."

Moments later, Audri had lighted the seven candles on her daughter's pink birthday cake, and she invited the ten little girls and Bradley and Brendan to start singing. In the voice of Grover, Kate ordered everyone to sing louder.

When "The Birthday Song" was over, Audri Stevens scolded her younger children. "Kate, I told you not to talk like a monster today!"

"But Bradley said I could as long as I didn't say Goddamnit anymore."

"Oh, no. Oh, Brendan! Why are you still wearing Mommy's makeup? I told you to go wash it all off, Son."

The young boy only pointed to his sister, who replied, "I told him to keep it on, because it's my birthday."

"Well, keep it on then, Son. But you can't have any cake and ice cream until you take it off." The boy bolted from the room to wash off his make up.

"He makes such a pretty girl, though!" Kate protested.

"Just eat cake, dear." Mrs. Stevens cut a piece and put it on a little paper plate.

Kate took the plate from her mother and shouted excitedly, "Cookie Monster eat cake!" She then proceeded to shove the entire portion into her mouth at once while muttering through the mass of it, "Yum yum yum yum yum!"

Bradley took the opportunity to slip out of the room, away from all of the insane little girls. He went to the phone and dialed Ann's number.

"Hello," came the harsh sound of Ann's mother's voice.

"Mrs. Maryweather. Hi! This is Bradley. May I please speak with Ann?"

"Ann isn't taking your calls, Bradley," the woman spoke frostily. "I think you'd better stay away from here from now on."

"But...she wasn't in school today. Is she sick?"

"Goodbye, Bradley. Don't call here again." A click and a dial tone followed her harsh words.

Bradley stood dazed for a long moment, before at last he slowly lowered the phone back down to the receiver. He was still in a daze when his mother came into the room.

"Oh, Bradley! I just don't know what to do with her! Who will ever want to marry a girl who talks like a sailor, or Cookie Monster for that matter! I'm trying so hard to set a good example."

Bradley spoke absently as he walked towards the stairs, "Mom, you're worrying about nothing. She's only seven."

"Oh, are you all right, dear?"

"Yeah," he said, as he began to climb the stairs. "I'm just fine."

It was dark by the time Ray returned to the hotel, and he had a lot on his mind; distracting things. He was glad. He had so much to keep him from thinking on dark secrets. He so wanted to get a good look at this mysterious Valen Alexas for himself. Tom's wife Abigail had slipped at dinner and told Ray what she wasn't supposed to. There had been another murder, and the body had been found in their own back yard. Tom had found it early that very morning. Ray was excited to have this to think on. The victim's throat had been ripped out, and there was another vampire picture in the victim's hand.

Ray turned the lock on his hotel room door and entered. Darkness surrounded him as he closed the door. He took a deep breath, looking forward to sleep, and he turned on the lights.

"Oh, fuck!" The room was trashed. The bed was turned over, his suitcase was empty, the contents spread across the room. The drawers were pulled from the night stand and the dresser, likewise emptied. The dresser and the night stand themselves were lying face down on the floor.

Ray covered his face with both hands and moaned loudly in outrage. "Oh, no! No! No!" He went into the bathroom and turned on the light. The lid was off of the toilet, the cabinets were opened. Towels lay everywhere. Ray hit the wall with his fist angrily several times. "Damn it! This is not happening!"

He looked up at the mirror, and he found something written there in red. Was it blood? He couldn't tell, and he didn't want to know. He wanted to hear from Lee now more than ever. He needed to know that Lee had gotten away. He read the message on the mirror aloud. "Genesis 6:4" He puzzled over it. "What the hell?"

Ray left the bathroom and searched the mess of his room for the hated Gideon's Bible, repeating the verse over and again to himself until he had uncovered the book and looked up the chapter. He read aloud, "'There were giants in the earth in those days; and also after that, when the sons of God came in unto the daughters of men, and they bare *children* to them, the same *became* mighty men which *were* of old, men of renown.'"

Ray dropped the Bible to the floor and turned red with rage, remembering the words of the man, or whatever it was, that he had been confronted by in Ireland; the being that had followed him there: Christian Rivers.

"I'm Christian Rivers of the Nephilim. We just want to help you out. We aren't like the Sions, but we know what you have. They will try to take it from you at any cost. It's their most precious secret. They'll do anything to protect it, you see. If you come with me now, the Nephilim will protect you. We've stood against Sion for ages. I don't want to see things get ugly for you. None of us do."

Ray had never let the man, or whatever it had been, finish its pitch. He had taken off with his treasure, against the seemingly benevolent warning. He couldn't make any arrangements without Lee, and he had lost his faith in everyone else. Why should he trust some other order? They were probably liars too. And now it seemed that his suspicions had been justified. "Lying, inhuman fucks!" For, now the Nephilim, who had claimed to have his best interests at heart when they'd sent Christian Rivers to follow him, seemed to have dropped the pretense. They had made it known that they were no less dangerous than the Order de Sion had been.

Ray slumped down to the floor. When he had just been on the run from one supposedly extinct secret society, it had been a laugh. Now there were two of them, natural enemies, united to take what was his. So much for being distracted.

Ray found a book of matches lying on the floor beside him, and he began to laugh. He took a match out and struck it against the little matchbook, watching the flame come to life. He then put the infant fire to the corner of the Gideons' little contribution to the mass brainwashing of the Christian world, and he watched the fire grow. He picked the burning book up by a corner, and he took it to the bathroom, where he tossed it into the tub and watched it burn. Ray giggled as the blaze consumed the book, its golden glow reflected in his glistening eyes. When the book was no more than a pile of ash, Ray turned on the shower to douse it. He then fell to the floor again and started to laugh uncontrollably. All that trouble, and they still hadn't taken it from him.

"If you're listening, Christian, you prick, I don't have it! I don't have it, and neither does Lee, and neither do you!" He laughed himself to tears. And soon the tears took on a life of their own. Ray screamed at the top of his lungs to break his dark train of thought. He screamed until he was out of breath.

Valentinus Alexas met Reverend Michaels at the front door of Nightfire United Methodist Church. "Thank you for meeting me so late, sir."

"Not a problem, Mr. Alexas. Your situation is rather unique, after all. Let's not waste any time. And by the way, call me Bob."

"Very well, Bob. And I am Valen."

"You shortened it. That's clever." The reverend unlocked the glass door and opened it.

"Clever?"

"I've been in Nightfire too long, Valen. Nothing gets by me. You've got nothing to worry about though. I keep everybody's secrets. If I wasn't good at it, you know the mayor would have gotten me out of this church as quickly as possible, by any means necessary."

Valen couldn't help but sound nervous with a stranger claiming to know his secrets. "Of course." But it was true. The pastor of Nightfire UMC was traditionally the guardian of the town's deepest secrets. There was no avoiding it; for they were buried deep within the church itself.

Bob Michaels, a short, round, balding, gray-haired man of fifty-seven, led the way with a limp to the stairs. He cackled as he descended them, and Valen followed warily.

Reverend Michaels opened the door to a closet in the large church basement, and he went in. "This is it, Valen. Your guardian angel in a jar." He cackled some more.

Valen entered the closet and breathed a sigh of relief at the sight of the glass beaker in the preacher's hand. "Thank God. I just needed to be sure. It helps me to sleep. I just needed to know that they couldn't get to me here."

"Sure can't. They've been kept away since August of 1850."

"Yes, my friend assured me that he could smell it at the border, ever so slightly."

"By my understanding, ever so slightly is more than enough to keep 'em out. You're friend, is he one of 'em?"

Valen laughed at this. "No. Not exactly. Well...let's just say I don't have to worry about him. He got me here safely. He's the only one who could."

"Interesting. I was thinking it odd that one of their own would be a friend of yours. Werewolves tend to band together. If you have one werewolf on your back, you have the whole pack on your trail."

Valen shivered. "Yes. I know, but he isn't...never mind that. I'd rather not get into it now. We shall just leave it that he is the truest of true friends. And they fear him, as they should."

"So, how did you get mixed up with werewolves, if you don't mind my asking? What did you do to turn them against you?" He placed the beaker back on the shelf.

Valen smiled and spoke softly, "But I do mind. It goes back a long way. Is that the document?"

Bob looked at the book beneath the beaker of blood. "Oh, yeah. Reverend Paul's book. The document's in it."

"May I...?"

"Sure thing." The reverend gently removed the beaker from its resting place and set it aside. He then took the book from the shelf and blew the dust from it before handing it over to Valen.

Valen regarded the book reverently, and he opened it directly to the pages that he sought. "*The Werewolf Plague of 1850.* The account of the pastor who lived through it and captured the werewolf blood from the devilish pack leader. The man who saved Nightfire for all these years by putting the blood in that very beaker. I am in debt to him. Some time, I would like to read this, perhaps to copy it." He closed it and handed it back to Bob carefully.

"I think that can be arranged, since you already know about that particular little secret. I assume you know quite a few more as well, if my suspicions are correct, and you have yet to deny that they are. But you must realize, the town government is very nasty when it has to be. These secrets are not to get out."

"Yes, I know. I...lived here before, as you know."

"Yes, I know." The minister seemed suddenly alarmed. "Oh, rats! I left the door upstairs unlocked!"

Valen smiled. "That's all right, Bob. Raksha's got it covered. She's my devoted beast. She's waiting for me and won't let anyone in, I assure you. Besides, it's time I took my leave. We don't want to be noticed."

"Right. So when do you want to come back and read it?"

"I don't know. I have to take care of some things first. I'll call you. Thank you for your cooperation, Bob. I will send a donation to your church."

"Much obliged, Valen. See you around."

"Yes. You will." Valen, still smiling, turned and walked away.

Bob stood in the basement alone, marveling at the things he'd seen since he'd arrived in Nightfire, Texas. Valen the latest of them all: the head of Alexas Enterprises. That and so much more.

***

Bradley Stevens and Samuel Turner took their seats at the bar in the center of Dan Parker's. Sam ordered for both of them. "Two Dr. Peppers, please." He set the money down on the counter.

The bartender, Victoria Parker, a lovely brunette with full and curly hair, took pity on Bradley. "What's the matter, hon? You need some cheerin' up?"

"It 's okay, girl. I got 'im," Sam said.

Ignoring Sam, Bradley looked up at Victoria, "Have you seen Ann today, Vicky? Or anybody else, like Dori or Mati?"

"No, I sure haven't. She hasn't done you wrong, has she?"

Bradley held his head in his fists, resting on his elbows, and he looked down at the bar. "I don't know."

She set the drinks down in front of the two boys. She looked at Sam and pushed his money away. "Here; you cheer him up and it's on the house." She winked at him.

"Thanks." Sam looked at his friend. Bradley had called and needed to talk. He had told Sam all about the phone conversation with Ann's mother, and how he didn't know what he should do. Sam felt bad, because he didn't know what to tell him. They had come to Dan Parker's in hopes that they would run into somebody who knew what was going on with Ann. Unfortunately, it was late, and most of Ann's friends were probably getting ready for bed.

A voice came from behind them. "Hey! Fancy meeting y'all here!"

Sam turned. "Hey, Ray! What's up, man?"

Bradley, hearing Ray's name, snapped out of his daze and turned around. He waved slightly with three of his fingers.

"What's with him?" Ray asked.

"Ann ain't speakin' to 'im. We don't know why," Sam answered.

Ray pointed to an empty table. "Come on, let's get a table! Hey, Vicky! Bring me a Dr. Pepper! I can't afford to get drunk tonight."

"Sure thing, Ray!" She shook her head and prepared his drink.

After Ray had received his beverage, and the other boys had joined him at a little round table in the front of the building, Ray looked after Victoria. "She wants me. You should have seen her when Tom and I stopped off for a beer earlier this evening. She couldn't keep her eyes off me."

"You really are arrogant, aren't you, Ray?" Sam said.

"It's well earned, my young friend." Ray laughed. "So, Bradley, what happened? Tell me, man. I need a distraction."

"From what?" Bradley asked without caring.

"From...things."

Sam's eyes grew wide, as he looked to the door. "How's that for a distraction, bro?" He raised his hand and waved at the man who'd just entered the bar and grill. "Yo, Valen! Over here!"

Valen smiled when he recognized Sam. He walked over to the little table, and Raksha followed. "Sam! I'm so pleased to see you again. I was hoping I would find you tonight."

Ray took a sip of his drink and said sardonically, "Better invest in turtle necks, Sam."

Sam just glared at Ray, not at all sure how to respond. He knew to the core of his being that Valen was not a bad guy.

"Hey, mister!" Victoria shouted from the bar. "Your pet's gonna have to wait outside!"

"Oh. It's all right. She won't bother anyone."

"No," Vicky said irritably, "it's not! We have rules here, you know!"

Valen knew Nightfire. He knew that rules of this kind only applied to strangers, and were easily bent for friends. He pulled out a hundred dollar bill. "There is a great deal of appreciation in it for you, if you'll let her stay. And you have my word that she'll behave."

Victoria laughed out loud. "Sure thing, love. Whatever you say." She went back to her work.

Ray spoke again. "She'd better invest in turtle necks too."

Valen looked at Ray as though he were a painting. His eyes were unblinking, and he seemed quite taken. "Raymond Aleister Don."

"How did you know my name, you freak?"

Valen pulled something out of his coat pocket. "You left your wallet in front of my house this afternoon. I was hoping to track you down. It's good fortune that I've found you *and* Sam."

"Well I guess it all depends on your perspective."

Bradley was drawn out of his stupor by the tension building between Ray and Valen. He had forgotten his earlier troubles and realized that a possible killer was about to sit at their table and perhaps even join them for a drink.

Samuel was just nervous, because he liked Valen. He wanted Ray and Bradley to know that Valen was okay. "Why don't you sit down, Val?"

Valen regarded Ray. "If it's not going to put anyone out."

Ray sat back and held up his hands. "Oh, no! I needed a distraction tonight! This is it! Sit!"

Valen pulled out a chair and took a seat. He smiled at Bradley.

Ray shouted to Victoria, "Hey, Vicky! Bring us another Dr. Pepper!"

Valen seemed taken by surprise. "Oh, no! Thank you but, I never drink," he paused and considered his words, "Dr. Pepper."

Ray stared at Valen for a long moment, then he rolled his eyes in disgust. "Okay! He's a psycho!" He shouted back to the bartender, "Never mind! He only drinks blood!"

Valen stood abruptly. "I'm sorry. It seems I've chosen a bad time to intrude."

Sam spoke up, "Valen, wait! He just can't help but piss people off. It's a personality disorder. He can't help it!"

"Oh! Right, Sam!" Ray protested. "So when this guy turns into a bat and flies away, is that what you're gonna call it? A personality disorder?"

"If you have something to say to me, Mr. Don, then do so. No need to hold back, sir."

Ray looked up at Valen and smiled madly, as though he were meeting Damnation and laughing it in the face. "All right. I think you're the Vampire Killer. I think you let your ugly pet there rip people open, and you put a picture in their hands, thinking that life is just like *Scooby-Doo*, and you have to leave your corny, little clues, so that we all think it's a vampire! I mean, come on, 'I never drink...Dr. Pepper.' That is the most blatantly vampiric thing that I have ever heard anyone say in my life! Don't tell me you didn't think that one through!"

Valen's face was like stone, devoid of emotion. "I see. I am sorry you feel this way, Mr. Don. But I am telling you, I am not this serial killer. I am Valen Alexas, the head of Alexas Enterprises. I am here to kick back for a while and restore the old Alexas mansion. I hope that, in time, you'll come to trust me. I hope that, in time, we can be friends." He turned to Sam. "Samuel. I have a proposition for you. Raksha seems to like you, and I anticipate that Mr. Don is not the only person in town who is going to try to pay me a visit when I'm...away. I am usually otherwise occupied during the day, and I leave Raksha to guard the house. It would be better for my windows and my future relations with the people of this town, if there were someone else there during the day; someone who can speak with visitors on my behalf and keep Raksha in line. I would pay you very well."

Samuel was surprised. "Well..."

Ray put a hand over the younger man's mouth and answered for him. "He'll think it over, Vlad. Now go on, and don't kill anybody I know." He took his hand off of Sam's mouth.

"Actually," Sam said angrily, "I *would* like to think it over first, and I could've told you so myself."

Valen nodded. "I'm glad that you will consider it. Now, please excuse me. I fear that I have disrupted the atmosphere here, and I do have...other matters to attend to. Good night." He bowed slightly and left the building, followed by his loyal wolf.

Sam was ticked off. "Don't ever speak for me, Ray!"

"I'm sorry. I just didn't want you to rush into anything."

"Well I'm not stupid! I never rush into things!"

"I'm sorry!"

"Good. I forgive you." Sam took a big gulp of his drink.

Bradley spoke as though he'd just been awakened from a dream, "Man, Ray. You're dead! That guy's vicious! And you called him a bad *Scooby-Doo* episode to his face!" Bradley began to laugh in amazement at the entire scene.

"Well," Sam ventured, "he said he wasn't the serial killer."

"Oh, yeah," Ray said. "And we all know that serial killers are legendary for their honesty."

"Don't be a smart ass, Ray. I'm serious. I just have a good feelin' about 'im. He can't be the serial killer."

"Well," Ray regarded the money that Valen had left by his wallet on the table. "I'd have a good feeling about a guy who leaves hundred dollar tips for absolutely nothing too, if he'd just offered me a job as his house boy."

"Ray," Bradley interjected. "Cool down, man! You're going off on Sam! You're going too far."

"I'm sorry." He looked them both in the eyes. "I really mean it. I'm sorry. I've had a really bad day, and I'm taking it out on the world I guess."

"That's okay, Ray," Sam said. "We all have bad days." He forced himself to grin, and then he found it genuine.

Bradley was still concerned. "Ray, you might have just made yourself the serial killer's next target! What were you thinking? This guy could be dangerous."

"Well," he gulped down the last of his Dr. Pepper, "Bradley, that's just the kind of excitement I've been looking for. Seems I'll have no choice other than to ponder it all night." He giggled and held up his glass. "Hey, Vicky! How 'bout a refill!"

I can't believe this! Audri Stevens was in miserable pain, as she walked outside towards the car. *I'll have to hurry, so that the children don't miss me.* She was suffering from a terrible headache, and Bradley was nowhere to be found. She had to go get some aspirin from the convenience store. Fortunately she had already put Brendan and Kate to bed, so they would never know that they'd been left at home alone. She dug in her purse for the car keys. She pulled them out, but was stopped from unlocking the door by a sound. She turned to find it.

No one was there. She turned back to the car and tried to turn the difficult lock. Just as she finally got it to click, she noticed a reflection in the window and gasped. "Oh!" She caught herself. "Bradley, Halloween is still three weeks away." She turned to face him. "I have to go to the...you're not..."

The man put a hand over her mouth and turned her around, pulling her close to him so that he was behind her. She felt something sharp at her throat, and she began to struggle. She felt his breath on her neck, as he whispered, "Don't scream."

CHAPTER 3
VICTORY OF THE VAMPIRE

It was 2:00 A.M. by the time Bradley had dropped Sam and Ray off and was headed home himself. He was more than ready for bed, and yet he didn't see himself getting any sleep this night. So many things were racing through his mind. He was miserable over the strangeness he was being put through with Ann. Well, Ann's mother anyway. He felt that his head might burst if he didn't get some answers. Why wouldn't she speak to him? What had gone wrong? Of course, it was clear that things were going to be different between them since they'd decided to make love, but why should it drive her away? It had been her idea in the first place.

Bradley was also concerned about this mysterious Valen Alexas. It was very possible that Ray had been correct. Valen could be Nightfire's serial killer. Which meant that Ray was in trouble, and so was Sam, for both had opened themselves to further contact with the man. And Ray had been bold enough to accuse him to his face. Bradley hoped that Ray was wrong, and that the whole thing would blow over. He thought about his father and his older brother, and then he considered this serial killer. He considered Ann. He breathed out a sigh and spoke to himself softly. "I just couldn't stand to lose anybody else right now."

A thought suddenly struck him as he turned onto his street. "I hope Mom didn't wait up." He snickered to himself. He hadn't intended to stay out so late, but the comfort and the conversation of his friends had been so wonderfully addictive.

Bradley pulled up slowly to his driveway. *That's funny*, he noted. *The lights are on inside Mom's car. Oh, shit!* A pair of legs had come into view, laying outstretched beside the car. Bradley stopped the car in front of the driveway, turned it off, and bolted out to his mother's car.

"Mom! Mom!" He ran to her side, fearing the worst. He knelt down beside her and shook her, only to scream out in horror at the site of her shredded throat. "Oh, God! Oh, fuck!" Bradley felt numb all over. He was sobbing before his next heartbeat, and, indeed every heartbeat seemed now to last an eternity. He was praying silently, begging God to wake him from this nightmare. *Maybe she's still alive. Maybe she's okay.* He closed his burning eyes and took a deep breath before again braving a look at her. Her skin was pale like snow, and her beautiful green eyes were staring wide with fear, not seeing anything; and never to see again. Bradley was trembling violently. He couldn't think. He sobbed, and he reached down to take her hand, and found it holding a card. He knew exactly what had happened. He pulled his hand away and fell on his backside. "Oh, God...," he murmured, just before he keeled over and vomited in the grass. Bradley had never felt shock quite like this; not when his father had died from a heart attack in the hospital; not even when his brother had been sent home in a box from Vietnam. This was the greatest horror he had ever known.

"Bradley!"

The voice of his little sister shocked him again, back to the rest of the world. "Fuck! Kate! Stay in bed!" He looked around frantically for her, and was relieved to find that she was calling from her bedroom window. She couldn't see her mother from that particular angle. "Just go to sleep, Kate!"

"But you were screaming. What's wrong?"

A light caught Bradley's eyes, as his little brother's bedroom window began to glow. Bradley was frantic. "Fucking go to sleep! I just tripped, I'm okay. Tell Brendan to get the fuck back to bed! Now!"

"Do you need me to get Mom?"

Bradley felt his heart split. "Oh, God. Fuck...no! No! I'm all right! I'll be upstairs in a minute to tell you all about it. And you and Brendan better fucking be in bed with all the lights out, or I'll tell...I'll...I'll just tell. Fuck! Put Brendan in bed!"

The little girl's voice rang out in irritation, "Fuck! I will! Watch your filthy fucking mouth!"

Satisfied that his sister was on task, Bradley tried not to look at the body before him. He needed to get moving. He needed to act. But then, he *needed* to look at her again. He needed to be sure. Maybe he had seen wrong. Maybe he had been tricked by the light. He looked down into her lifeless eyes; he glanced over her ivory white skin. "Oh, God!" He felt dizzy, as he rocked back and forth on his haunches. "Move, Bradley. Do something. Fucking move!" He banged a fist on the side of his mother's car, and he let out a defiant scream, as he rose to his feet, still weeping. He marched, quivering with terror, over to the neighbors' house, and he started to pound on the door.

Mr. Jones opened the door in his robe a few minutes later, put on his glasses, and took in the disheveled sight of Bradley. "Bradley! What's the matter, son?"

Bradley couldn't make himself speak for a moment. His eyebrows rose, and his lips began to tremble. He took in a shaky breath and blurted out meekly, just before breaking into sobs again, "My Mom's dead."

Suddenly Mr. Jones was all the strength Bradley was so desperate for. He grabbed the youth and held him close, letting the boy soak his shoulder with his tears. His wife had quietly emerged from the shadows behind him. "Carl, what's happened?"

Mr. Jones barely turned his head to regard his wife. "I need you to call the police and send them over to the Stevens' house."

Her eyes went wide. "What...?"

"Please, Dear, hurry. Then go see that Eleanor hasn't been frightened by the knocking." She looked at him, clearly frightened, but needing to understand more. "Mrs. Stevens needs help."

"Oh. Oh, my! I'll call Will Cody at home." She hurried off, dragging the phone, as she spoke into it, over to their four year old daughter's bedroom door.

While Mrs. Jones was on the phone, Carl led Bradley into the kitchen and sat him down at the table. "Bradley, what happened? Tell me, son."

Bradley looked up in agony. "She's...someone did this. Someone hurt her bad." He spoke in a near whisper through phlegm he hadn't the will to clear, "It's the killer." Carl's eyes went wide, just as Bradley's did, and the young man jumped up. "Brendan and Kate!"

Carl put a hand on the youth's shoulder and pushed him gently back to his seat. "I'll go for them, Bradley. Are they all right?"

"Yes. Kate was talking through her window, asking me what was wrong...I didn't tell her."

"That was wise."

"Brendan's light came on, but I didn't hear him say anything." Suddenly the possibility that it hadn't been Brendan who'd turned on the light dawned on both men, and their faces showed it. "Oh, God! He could be in the house! He could be in there with my brother!" Bradley stood back up. "I have to get them out!"

"No!" Mr. Jones spoke sternly. "You're in no condition. I'll go."

"Go where?" Asked Mrs. Jones, who'd just walked into the kitchen carrying their sleeping daughter.

"Susan, did you get the police?"

"Yes. What's going on, Carl? I'm scared."

Mr. Jones said nothing at first, looking down, considering how much to tell his wife at this moment. "Susan, don't worry. I'm going next door to get Brendan and Kate. Lock the door behind me, and don't open it until I knock and you know for sure it's me."

Susan was getting irritated. "Carl..."

Bradley spoke up. "Go through the back. You can't take them through the front. Please, I don't want them to see her." The young man looked pleadingly to his neighbor.

"Carl, what is wrong with Audri?" She took in the silence, the way that her husband avoided her eyes, the positively stricken look of young Bradley Stevens, and her intuition kicked in. "Oh my God. Carl, wait for the police! They'll get the kids out. You can't go over there, he might still..."

Carl cut her off sharply. "He might still be in there, and I'll never sleep again if I just stand by and wait for the police while that monster butchers those little children. Lock the doors. I'll be right back." Carl opened the sliding glass door to their back yard, and he picked up a baseball bat. He kissed his wife gently on the lips, and he kissed his daughter on the head, then he headed out. Susan locked the door and closed the drapes, holding her daughter tightly.

Bradley felt his mind slipping. He just knew that he would never get over this. He kept drifting to practical thoughts, then stopping himself, not wanting to be in this moment. *How are we gonna eat? I suppose I could…*

How am I gonna pay for a funeral? I'll have to call…

How am I gonna tell Brendan and Kate? God…

Bradley stood abruptly and started pacing in the small kitchen, nearly oblivious to the presence of the mother and daughter just beside him.

"Bradley," Susan offered, "I'm so sorry."

He stopped pacing and regarded Mrs. Jones as though she were the strangest thing he'd ever seen.

"I'm so glad you came to us. If there's…if there's anything we can help with…I just want you to know that you have friends here, Bradley."

The youth considered her words, then managed to choke out a, "Thank you." He had to stop speaking then, for fear of losing control of his tears. He passed the minutes by in agony, wanting it all to end.

There was a knock on the door, and Mrs. Jones jumped. "Oh!"

"I'll go look," Bradley insisted. He went to the back door and peeked through the curtains. It was Mr. Jones, and his brother and sister. Bradley felt such relief as he threw back the curtains and opened the sliding glass door, that he almost shouted aloud.

The three entered the house, and Mr. Jones closed the door behind him. "Everybody's here, Susan. Let's make some hot chocolate."

"Yeah!" Came little Eleanor's enthusiastic shout from her mother's arms. "What's going on, Mommy?"

Bradley knelt down and embraced his young siblings tightly.

"Bradley," Brendan asked, "what is going on?" The boy looked scared, as though, deep down inside, he already knew what Bradley was holding back.

Still, he didn't look nearly as frightened as Kate. "Where's Mom?" she blurted. Bradley could see she was on the verge of tears. She knew something was terribly wrong.

Bradley sat back, his eyes began to water, and he blinked rapidly, trying to speak through the pain in his throat. "Look, guys…um…something happened…" He stopped and stood, interrupted by the sounds of a police siren and the flashing of lights through the window.

"What's happening?" Asked Eleanor, still refused answer by her clearly frightened mother.

"Everybody sit still," came the calming voice of Carl Jones. "I'm gonna go talk to the police officers, and we'll clear everything up when I get back." He looked to Bradley. The boy looked as though he were ready to burst through the wall to get out there. "Bradley, you wanna come outside with me, or do you wanna wait here till I come back?"

"I'm coming with you." Bradley hurried to the front door, and he was outside before Mr. Jones had even managed to leave the kitchen.

***

"Oh my god." Dirk was standing beside the body of Audri Stevens. He looked to Sheriff Cody.

"Looks like our Poker game wasn't interrupted for nothin' after all," came the sheriff's reply. "My God…Audri. Those poor kids. They've been through Hell and back already. Now this."

Dirk knelt down for a closer look. "There's something in her hand."

"Well, that figures, Dirk. There's been somethin' in all their hands."

"Sheriff Cody!"

Will Cody looked to see Bradley Stevens running at him from the Jones' house, followed by Carl. "Bradley, stay back, son."

Carl shouted, "You're not gonna be able to stop that kid if you run 'im over with a bus. He's the one who found 'er, Sheriff."

Sheriff Cody's heart sank at the revelation. How tragic for that poor boy, who'd known so much pain in his life already. "I'm sorry, son. All we can do is find whoever did this and see that he gets what's comin'."

Anger filled Bradley's whole being, and he thought back to Ray's accusations at Dan Parker's. "Then arrest Valen Alexas! He's the one! He's the killer! He has to be!"

The sheriff wanted to hear more, but he had to treat anything relating to Valen Alexas with special caution. "Why's that, Bradley? Did you see somethin'?"

Bradley was growing frustrated, and he spoke through gritted teeth, fists clenched at his sides, "No...but...he has a wolf."

The sheriff still wanted to hear more, but his curiosity remained apprehensive. "Look, son. It's complicated. I got a visit from the mayor on account of Mr. Alexas stayin' in our town. Now, I'm not sayin' I'm necessarily gonna comply, but he gave me and my department a strict order to stay outa Valen Alexas' way. Said it had somethin' to do with agreements signed with the town's founders a hundred-aught years back." He saw the outrage on the youth's face. "Now, I *will* look into this, son. If there's a chance Valen Alexas is a cold blooded killer, then to Hell with the mayor's order. I'm learnin' more an' more that this town is just plain peculiar. There's special allowances left an' right. The town government ain't even like most towns. There was some weird shit goin' on back in the last century whenever *who*ever put this town together, and there's a lota secrets. That makes me plenty uncomfortable, 'cause I ain't privy to any of 'em. All I know's that we have to be careful how we handle Valen Alexas. Sheriff Gilespe violated an order from the mayor like this, and next thing ya know feds are all over 'im. Now he's in the nut house. Like I said, I don't know what this secret contract's all about, but I know better than to stick my dick in it."

Bradley wasn't the least bit impressed. "Look, he has a wolf! I know that you've found wolf hair at the scene of each murder! Nobody else in Nightfire has a wolf! People have seen him. He walks around with it. I saw him just tonight at Dan Parker's. He had the wolf with him then! These murders started as soon as he got here! You have to do something, or he's gonna just keep killing!"

"If you saw him and the wolf at Dan Parker's…"

"He left a long time before I did. You can ask Sam and Ray. He said he had some business to take care of or something! Please, Sheriff Cody! You have to do something tonight! My Mom!" Bradley pointed, without looking, to the spot where Audri lay. He covered his face.

Sheriff Cody could no longer look the boy in the eyes anyway. "Look, Bradley. I know you're hurtin', but the fact is, we need more to go on. We don't have anything at *this* crime scene to point the finger at Valen Alexas, 'cept some half crazy, grief-struck kid. You need to be patient and let *us* figure this one out."

Bradley stomped past the Sheriff. "Fuck you then!" He got in his car and started the ignition.

"Now hold on a minute, son! Where in Hell do ya think yer goin'?"

Without reply, Bradley hit the gas, squealing the tires as he drove away.

"God damn it!" Will Cody shouted at the top of his lungs. "Where in Hell is that kid goin' off to?"

"Sheriff," Carl offered, worry in his voice, "if that were your mother laying there on the pavement, and you thought you knew who did it, where would *you* be headed right now?"

Will thought for a moment. "Shit. You don't think that kid'd be crazy enough to…this is nuts! I hate shit like this! Nightfire's s'posed to be a nice, quiet little town; so why does this weird shit always come up! We don't even have anything here that *points* to Valen Alexas."

"Uh…Sheriff?" came Dirk's worried voice.

"What is it, Dirk?"

The younger man held something up in his hand. "It's wolf's hair, sir. Same species as at the other scenes."

"Well, shit in my Corn Flakes! I guess we have to go retrieve Bradley, before he gets himself killed. Why couldn't I have at least been *winnin'* that Poker game before we came out here? It never fails; when it rains, it pours."

Bradley sped down the dirt road leading to Alexas Mansion and slammed on the brakes right at the front porch. He turned off the ignition, slammed the door, and marched up the stairs. For the entirety of the drive, Bradley had been of only one mind—the mind of vengeance. His mother was dead, and he would havc satisfaction with her killer.

All the first floor lights were on, which didn't surprise Bradley at all. He stood at the door, shaking slightly with anger, trying to collect himself, wondering just exactly what it was that he was going to do.

***

Inside, Valen, having seen to all his nightly tasks, was relaxing with a book, and giggling, in his living room. He was lounging in nothing but a white T-shirt and a brand new pair of bell-bottom jeans, which was not his normal style. He had been thinking about his wardrobe though, and he felt home was the best place to get comfortable with a new look. He knew that Julius would have mocked his paranoia, but Valen was worried that his other clothes made him look too old, and he wanted to look as young as possible. Perhaps it *was* as ridiculous as Julius thought, but Valen was always worried about how old he looked, one way or the other.

It was awkward at times, being in his unique situation. He was head of the corporate empire that was Alexas Enterprises, and yet he was so youthful. In business meetings, which he generally only sent a representative to, but sometimes couldn't avoid, Valen would always worry that he didn't look old *enough.* It wasn't easy gaining respect from men who saw him as a mere boy; the unappreciative, undeserving heir to the Alexas fortune. He knew that many of them saw him this way. He'd heard them speaking in the halls.

In Nightfire, however, it was the other way around. It wasn't respect he sought from the people here, but friendship. He worried that his overly mature mannerisms and all-business way of dressing would prevent him from fitting in with the young people he was most likely to click with. And he needed friends here, since he would surely be staying for a long time, and he wanted to have some semblance of normalcy. Though, he had to admit, he was anything but normal, which is why such things had always eluded him.

Valen finished a chapter, still giggling, and he put the book down. It was his favorite, even alongside all of all the classics he'd read, and it never failed to make him laugh. The book was called *Through Texas on a Mule*, and Valen had taken it with him on all of his own recent travels, relating to the main character, who wandered the state with his faithful yellow mule, just barely getting by and meeting a variety of strange people along the way. Valen thought about his old friend Tex McCoy, who he'd last seen in Amarillo. He worried, for surely his enemies would think to use his friends against him. But Julius had given his word to take care of the people Valen himself could no longer look after.

Valen looked over at Raksha, who sat alertly looking to an empty chair, as though someone were sitting in it. He was concerned about Raksha's behavior since they'd arrived in Nightfire. It was unnerving how she went about the house, every now and again seeming to react to the invisible. It wasn't something Valen wanted to think about in this great old house. The chair suddenly moved, ever so slightly, and a chill went through Valen, for he was sure his pet wolf hadn't touched it.

Then Valen's heart nearly leapt out of his chest, when he heard the thunderous, violent knocking at his front door. Raksha snarled and bolted to the front of the house. Valen quickly followed. He stood beside the growling wolf and looked through the peep hole. He was greatly relieved, and somewhat elated, to see one of Sam's friends; someone he'd hoped to get to know in time, after seeing him earlier that night at Dan Parker's, at the table with Sam and Ray.

Bradley saw the shadows approaching through the curtains by the door. He didn't care if this guy *ever* understood, he was just going to kill him. He had blind rage to back him now, and nothing would stand in his way. The more he thought it over, the angrier he became.

The locks turned, and the door opened slowly, revealing a quietly growling wolf, beside the brightly smiling vampire killer. Valen spoke with a welcoming voice, as though two or three in the morning was a wonderful time to have strangers pop by, "Hello! I didn't catch your name, but…"

"Catch this, mother fucker!" Before he even realized what he was doing, Bradley's fist met Valen's face and knocked the man back. Satisfaction only began to course through the young man's being as he made ready to hit him again, and again, and again…but Raksha wouldn't have that.

Before Bradley could even raise his fist again, the wolf was in the air; then Bradley was on the ground, the wolf on his chest. It was all a blur, and the sound of the beast's threatening snarl was all there was in the world. Then, "No! Raksha! Stop!" There had been panic in the man's voice, as though he didn't think the wolf would hear him. As the silence set in, only then, did Bradley realize that the monster's teeth were on his throat. The wolf had stopped less than an instant away from killing him. Somehow, Bradley didn't care. He was shocked, but he was undeterred.

The wolf backed up, slightly, still on Bradley's chest. It began growling again, as the boy stirred. "Raksha!" The man was pleading. "It's okay, girl. I can handle him."

Raksha looked to her master, as though to ask him, *Are you sure?* Valen nodded, and, after granting Bradley one more threatening show of her fangs, she turned and went to her master's side.

Bradley slowly raised himself up on his elbows and coughed, only just realizing that the wind had been knocked out of him. He spoke venomously, "I hate you. You bastard. I'm going to kill you."

Raksha began to growl again, ready to spring forth once more. Valen looked warningly at her and asked the youth nervously, "Why?"

Bradley sat up fully then, and he got to his feet, trying to look threatening, trying not to see the vicious wolf. "Because…the woman you…," he started to cry, and he detested himself for it, "…killed tonight. The woman you…ripped apart at the throat with your fucking pet wolf…she was my mother. You fuck! You killed my mother." Bradley stepped towards Valen, and the wolf snorted, but was cut short by an order from her master.

"Raksha," Valen spoke sternly, without even giving her a glance. "Go."

The beast looked stricken, insulted. Her eyes seemed to ask, *You* dismiss *me?* Still, she obeyed, and she walked sulking into the house, tail between her legs, as she melted into the shadows. Clearly, Raksha was not happy with the idea of leaving Valen to fend for himself. Clearly, she was well trained to protect him.

Valen stepped out onto the porch and stared directly into Bradley's glistening, teary eyes. Valen couldn't blame him for the accusation. He'd heard the reports himself. There was wolf hair found at the scene of each crime. As far as he knew, there were no other wolves in Nightfire. Of course this pointed to him. He had to act quickly. He had to escape suspicion. Of course, he was protected by the agreements made between the town founders in the early days of Nightfire, and he knew it, but if they didn't think he was standing by his part of the deal, surely they'd go over his head. Surely they'd protect themselves. Bradley's eyes went wide, locked to his own, and Valen knew that he had him.

Bradley felt an inner warmth come over him; a calm. Something in Valen's eyes. Something so…hypnotic. He didn't want to look away.

"What's your name?" Valen asked calmly.

"Bradley." Where was his anger? Bradley was dazed. He knew he should feel angry, but the anger wasn't there. All he wanted to do was answer Valen's question. "Bradley O'Denehy Stevens."

Valen smiled. "Well, Bradley O'Denehy Stevens, I'm glad to know your name. Now, you must listen to me. I know you're in pain. I lost my mother too…when I was very young." Pain crept into Valen's heart. This was not something he liked to think back on. In fact, because of how terribly she'd died before his eyes, Valen did not like thinking back on her at all. "You must believe me, Bradley. I killed no woman this night. I know Raymond accused me, and I see where you might suspect it, but I am not this serial killer."

Bradley let the words sink in. If ever there were a sound of truth, it was in Valen's smooth voice. Valen couldn't have killed his mother. It had to have been someone else. Bradley couldn't think clearly, though. All he could do was look into Valen's seductive, blue eyes. It was as if the eyes were speaking to him themselves, and they could have convinced him of anything. But, if Valen didn't kill his mother, who did? *My mother is dead.* This thought suddenly tore Bradley's eyes away from Valen's. He looked down and put a hand to his face as he sobbed. "My mom is dead!" He let out a growl of his own, sounding much more dangerous than the wolf in the shadows of the house. "Something has to be done!" He looked back to Valen, who was shedding silent tears, perhaps in sympathy. Or perhaps he was remembering his own mother's death. "My mom is dead, and I don't have anybody. What am I gonna do! How am I gonna take care of my brother and sister? What're we gonna do?" He broke down completely, repeating through sobs, "What're we gonna do?"

Valen went to the youth and held him. Bradley couldn't fight it. He needed to be held, by anyone. He couldn't remember what he'd come here for. He couldn't remember anything at the moment, except that his mother had been murdered...and Valen's magical eyes. Bradley got hold of himself then, and he let go of the older man and stood back, wiping his eyes and sniffling. He remembered why he'd come then. "I'm sorry…" he looked at the man and didn't quite know how to address him. Earlier the man had clearly looked like a Mr. Alexas, but now, he looked boyish, like a 'just Valen' sort of man, a little younger than Ray. "I'm sorry…Valen. I don't know how I could have thought…"

Valen put a hand on his shoulder. "It's okay, Bradley. I'd forgive you for anything the state you're in." He felt such a need to nurture this boy. He remembered the agony when he'd lost his own mother so long ago. Even though the circumstances had been greatly different, they were similar enough that Valen wanted to wash Bradley's pain away. He could easily imagine the sorrow that he felt.

Just then a police car drove up the road and parked beside Bradley's car. Both doors flew open, and Sheriff Cody and Officer Dirk stepped out, looking as all business as they could manage. Will Cody spoke cautiously. "Mr. Alexas…Bradley…Everything alright here?" His hand hovered by his gun, and he didn't care if it was obvious.

Bradley spoke, as Dirk went boldly up the steps of the porch beside him, "Sheriff Cody! I'm sorry. I made a mistake. I fucked up."

The two law men exchanged suspicious glances. The sheriff said, "I just wanna be sure, Bradley. What changed your mind?"

This question seemed to startle Bradley, as though he had never considered that before. "I…" He looked to

Valen. "I don't know. I just know it wasn't Valen. It couldn't have been."

Dirk spoke up, "Mr. Alexas…"

"Valen, please."

Dirk indulged the man. "Valen…do you mind if I take a look at your wolf?"

At this, Sheriff Cody actually put his hand on his gun and gripped it, ready to pull it from its holster in an instant if the need arose.

Valen regarded the police officer on his porch. He knew this could be trouble, and his nervousness showed. He wasn't sure how he would react if they took Raksha, or if they decided to arrest him. All he knew was that he would not allow himself to be taken into custody under any circumstances. And he knew that these policemen knew nothing about the agreement that protected him, or else they'd have steered clear, fearing for their very lives if anything should happen to him. For now, all Valen could do was play along and hope it didn't come to that. He called nervously into the house. "Raksha! Come here, girl."

The wolf came quickly, eager to get a closer look at the new arrivals; eager to size them up. She'd been eavesdropping long enough. Valen gave her a look that spoke volumes. Volumes which only the wolf could read. "Raksha, girl. Introduce yourself to this nice policeman."

The wolf looked up at Valen, understanding in her golden eyes, and she walked over to Dirk. He kneeled down and rubbed her neck. "Hey, you're a pretty girl, aren't you?"

As Dirk sat admiring the beast, Sheriff Cody started to lose his patience. "You live alone here, Valen?"

Valen regarded him with forced calm. "Just me and the dog, sir."

"That's not a dog, son. That's a wolf. And there's a vast, unfriendly difference between the two. A wolf ain't nothin' like a dog, 'cept maybe in looks. Wolves are killers. And you may have heard, we've got ourselves a killer in Nightfire."

Dirk spoke up, "Wolves are smarter too. My sister Sheryl works with wolves up in New Mexico. She tells me they have to put locks on all the pins, because, unlike dogs, the wolves watch their keepers closely. They learn real fast how to open the pins themselves. They don't have to see a person do it more than twice. Dogs can see someone open the gate a hundred times without figuring it out." He regarded the wolf he still petted. "Isn't that right, girl? I bet you're smart." He looked to Valen. "Of course, this also means that the wolf is not easy to tame. How long have you had Raksha here?"

Valen answered, "Four years. I raised her from a pup."

"Well, she seems friendly enough, tame enough, but I know for a fact, it's all just an act. You can't make a dog out of a wolf, man. No matter how housebroken she is, she's still a wild animal." He stood and spoke to the sheriff. "These facts considered, Raksha still hasn't gone near any of the murder victims."

Sheriff Cody stammered, not having expected that declaration from Dirk. "What're you talkin' about, Dirk! How can you say that fer sure just by lookin' at it?"

Dirk shrugged as he walked down from the porch. "She's the wrong species of wolf. We're looking for a red wolf. Raksha here's a gray wolf. You know my sister's in town, staying with my parents, right? She identified the wolf hair for me a couple days ago. She researches wolves for a living."

Sheriff Cody was irritated. "Damn it, Dirk, why didn't you say so earlier?"

"We didn't have a suspect earlier. Now we know. There has to be another wolf. And it has to be a pet wolf. 'Cause, I know wolves are smart, but no wolf is gonna be smart enough to put a picture of a movie vampire in each of the victims' hands."

"Damn it, Dirk! What's wrong with you, son! Next time, you tell me all the unimportant details 'soon as you know 'em."

"Yes, sir. Sorry." He grinned, clearly impressed with himself.

The sheriff looked up to the porch. "Sorry to trouble you, Mr. Alexas. I hope Bradley didn't wake you."

"No." Valen was laughing with relief. "I' m something of a night owl anyway."

"Bradley," the sheriff added, "come on back with us now, son. Brendan and Kate need you right now."

Bradley nodded his head, gave Valen a confused look, a silent farewell. Something had passed between them, but Bradley didn't understand it at all. He just knew that he felt safe with Valen. He felt like he knew him now, even though he really knew nothing about the man. Bradley got in his car after the law men got in theirs, and he drove off towards home. The last place he wanted to go.

Valen put a hand on Raksha's head and breathed a sigh of relief, as he whispered, "That was close."

Mary found Sam immediately after school let out that afternoon. "Sam! Did you hear?"

He turned from his locker and regarded her somberly. "'Bout Bradley's momma? Yeah. That's just awful. I only just met 'im, you know? I really don't know what to do. I went out with him last night, before it happened, and he was already real messed up over Ann." He shook his head. "I don't know why he wanted to confide in me. I don't know why he latched onto me so fast at all, but it makes me feel kinda responsible. Like I gotta watch his back. But I don't know what to say. I never knew nobody whose momma got killed. She was a real nice lady too." He remembered her bandaging him and Ray just two days before, telling him innocently enough about her youthful days…and Negro Fun Night. He laughed shortly. "Real nice."

Mary put a hand on his shoulder. "Oh, baby. You're such a good friend. I'm sure you'll know what to say, when you see him."

Sam stopped. "Baby?"

She just smiled.

"Girl, you just went out with me once, and we got chased away by a wolf. You sure you wanna call me your baby just now?"

She put a hand on his face and caressed him. "You're the cutest boy in school, Sam. Maybe it's wishful thinking on my part, but I…"

Sam interrupted quickly, "Aw, no! It ain't wishful thinking, Mary! You can call me your baby all you want!" He beamed. And she squealed.

As Sam continued to get the books he needed out of his locker, Mary recalled how he'd looked bothered when she'd seen him earlier. Intuition told her that something other than Bradley's mother was bothering him. "Sam?"

"Yeah?" He added a moment later, "Baby."

"Is there something else bothering you? I just get this feeling that there is."

Sam was impressed. "Well, yeah, as a matter of fact…" He closed his locker, holding only the books he would need to study over the weekend under his right arm. He then offered his left hand to her, she took it, and they walked down the hall. "It's just that, well, it seems I'm makin' friends real fast, which is good, especially considering that it didn't look too good for me when I first got here. But, I guess all this stuff with Valen is getting to me."

"Like what?"

"Well, like him an' Ray don't get along, and I know Valen's a good guy. I just get this feelin' about him. And, well, Valen offered me a job last night."

"What kind of job?"

"Well, that's the thing. It's like, watchin' his house and stuff after school, while he's away. Mainly 'cause of Ray goin' by there an' teasin' the wolf till it broke through a window and bit him in the ass."

Mary laughed at this. "Ray's such a charmer."

Sam rolled his eyes. "Tell me about it. Anyway, I really kind of think I want to do it, but I hadn't thought about any of the implications till this morning, when my Granny went off about the old days…again. See, in the old days, my Granny's own momma was a slave, right here in Nightfire. And guess who owned her."

Mary was very interested. "Who?"

"A man named Valentinus Alexas, who lived in that very same mansion that his descendant, Valen, lives in now."

"Oh, my God! That's so weird!"

"Yeah. I know. So, she's all tellin' me that, if I go take care of this man's house, I'll be undoing everything that the Civil War was fought for. I'll be selling our family back into slavery with the Alexases. But I just don't see it like that. That's crazy! It's just a typical high school kid job, ya know? Any white boy would take the job, right?"

She thought about it. "Well, yeah, probably."

"And there's a big difference in bein' a slave and house-sittin' for a few hours after school every day."

Mary cautioned him, "But, don't you think you should at least consider your Granny's feelings, Sam? Slavery was no small thing, after all. We're still suffering the aftermath of it all. The racism. The lack of education. I mean, we're some of the first black people to go to Nightfire High School. The scars of segregation are still fresh. The old school house we used to have to go to is still standing on the other side of Hill Park. You could get another after-school job that doesn't involve working in the house your family used to be slaves in."

"Yeah, but no other job gonna pay me ten dollars an hour."

"Ten dollars! Wow!"

"Hell, yeah! I know! And, aside from that, I really like Valen. I think he's cool. But I don't have to make up my mind right away." An inspired notion struck Sam then. "Hey, why don't you come with me to see him tomorrow night? He felt really bad about you having to jump out the window last time. I'm sure he'd love to meet you!"

Mary was reluctant. Maybe it was easy for Sam to get over being chased by a wolf, but for Mary it was asking a lot. Still, it meant spending time with Sam. "Sure…I'd love to. You're sure the wolf is tamed?"

Sam laughed at her fear. "Of course she's tamed. That's the coolest animal I've ever met! Smart as a whip!"

Mary smiled as Sam opened the door, and the pair walked out into the cool October afternoon.

At 10:30 that night, Bradley closed the door to his brother's room and faced Ray. Absolute exhaustion covered him like a shadow. "I think he'll be okay now. I just wonder how many more nights are gonna be like this, before it all seems normal."

"Time will tell," Ray said. He shook his head sadly. "I thought Kate would never calm down."

"Yeah. I don't know who's worse off right now, Brendan or Kate."

"Or Bradley."

The younger man shrugged Ray's comment off. "Ah, I'll be all right. I've lost family before."

"So? I've lost friends before. That doesn't make it easier, you know. Look, anything you need, Bradley…I'm there."

"I know, Ray. I really appreciate you staying with us for a while. I just…can't do this by myself right now."

"No problem, Bradley. Hey, she was like a mother to me too. And you're like a brother. Besides, the hotel was tired of me anyway." He grinned miserably.

"Yeah…well, you're okay on the couch?"

"Sure. No problem. I'll see you in the morning…I'm cooking. The kids'll love it."

"I'm sure, well…goodnight."

"'Night, Bradley."

With that, the two friends went in opposite directions. Bradley went to his room, and Ray went downstairs to the couch. He took off his shirt, grabbed a blanket, and lay down, thinking, as he did every night. It was good to be out of the hotel, after the mess his uninvited guests had made of it yesterday. He just wasn't feeling safe there anymore. Not that he felt great here. It was hard to be here, spending the night. So many things were missing. So many people. Ray had almost collapsed when he'd heard that Mrs. Stevens had been killed…and that Bradley had gone after Valen Alexas. Could Valen really be innocent? Ray didn't like to think so. Of course, he had his own reasons not to want *anybody* living in the Alexas Mansion. This was going to complicate things…but only slightly. It wasn't as though he could've kept things uncomplicated anyway. It was the very nature of his troubles.

A sound interrupted Ray's thoughts. It was a muffled, sobbing sound. He jumped up and went to the stairs, thinking one of the kids had lost it again, until he followed the sound to Bradley's room. He opened the door. "Bradley?"

The younger man looked up, tears flowing. "Ray…I'm sorry…I can't seem to cry enough."

Ray closed the door behind him. "Well, shit, Bradley! I'm not blaming you. I'd be crying too." He wanted to laugh at Bradley's pointless apology, but something stopped him. Perhaps just a rare moment of tact.

"Ray…my whole family is dying off. I'm the oldest one now. I can't raise Brendan and Kate…I still have to finish raising myself ."

Ray went to the bed, and he sat beside Bradley, putting an arm around him. "Hey, don't worry. We're gonna get through this together, man. You'll see. I'm with you all the way."

"Ray…I'm so glad you came back. I love you so much, you know. I really need a big brother right now, and you're a Godsend."

Ray was quiet. He didn't know what to say about being a Godsend. "I love you too, Bradley. I'm here for you no matter what." He held Bradley tight, until the younger boy fell asleep on his shoulder. Then, Ray fell asleep himself, wondering how he was going to be any help at all.

The following night, Sam and Mary drove out to the Alexas mansion as planned. Mary was still a little nervous. "Now, you're *sure* this wolf is tamed."

Sam laughed. "Yes! It's tamed. This is gonna be fun. You'll really like Valen. You'll see."

Mary parked her car, and the two of them got out. The lights were on, so Sam went up to the front door and knocked. After a minute, Mary said, "Are you sure he's home?"

Sam conceded, "Well, no, but, I got the impression he spent most of the night at home. We'll just wait another minute." He knocked some more, but there was not even the hint of Raksha in the house.

"So," Mary asked, a bit creeped out by the surrounding darkness of the trees and shrubs and land and shadows that surrounded the Alexas mansion, "did you ever talk to Bradley?"

"Yeah, I ran into Ray, and he'd been with Bradley all day. I helped Ray take his stuff from the hotel over to Bradley's house. I spent some time with them, before they had to get the kids to bed. Man, Ray's hotel room was trashed! The owner's gonna be pissed!"

"So, is he moving in for good, or what?"

"No. He's just stayin' till they figure out what they can do about Bradley's situation. Bradley was talkin' about quitting school."

"Oh, that's not good." Mary shook her head.

"I know." Sam was trying to make anything out through the drawn curtains on the windows. "I'm gonna go around back and see if he's there. It's a big house. He might just not hear us. Wait here, incase he comes to the door."

Mary didn't like that idea, but she agreed anyway. "Okay. Hurry."

"I will, baby. I'll be right back." He flashed a pearly-white smile and bounded down the stairs. In a moment, he'd disappeared around the corner.

Mary started to get antsy after a minute or so. She thought she heard something in the brush. "Sam?" *If he's trying to scare me, I'm gonna make him pay.* She left the porch and walked over to her car. She felt safer by the car than on that lonely porch. The car was like a friend in the darkness; something familiar. "Sam, what's taking so long?"

Mary was about to call louder, but she was prevented. A strong hand grabbed her from behind, covered her mouth. She felt something sharp at her neck, as the voice behind her whispered, "Don't scream."

Mary's eyes went wide with terror. This was it. This was the vampire killer who'd been in the paper, and tomorrow, she was going to be in the paper too. Mary tried to struggle, but the man was too strong for her. She felt the sharpness turn into a pressure on her tender neck, just as she heard that rustling in the brush getting louder. She turned her eyes, trying to make out what was creating the noise, only to see that devilish wolf leaping towards them. She braced herself for the end. She couldn't fight the man off. She couldn't call for help. The wolf was speeding towards her to tear her throat apart, and the man behind her was going to put a picture of a vampire in her hand when he was done. Tears were streaming down her face, as she begged in silent prayer to God.

And right at that moment, the wolf brushed past her, knocking the man off of her. Mary fell to the ground and felt her throat, where the sharpness had been about to puncture her. She heard a struggle. She turned to look, but she couldn't see anything. The fighting had moved out of range. She heard a man's voice, shouting, cursing. She heard the wolf snarling, jaws snapping. Then she heard the wolf cry out in pain. She screamed.

"Mary!" Sam came running. "What's wrong!"

Mary just got up and hugged Sam, pointing to where the sounds of struggle had gone silent.

At that instant, Valen Alexas appeared from the direction Raksha had bounded in from. "Sam! What's happened? Have you seen Raksha? She ran off a few minutes ago, and I couldn't get her to come back."

"No," Sam said, holding Mary. "And I don't know what happened."

"She saved me, Mr. Alexas. The killer had me. He had a knife or something at my throat."

Sam stood back. "Oh, my God!"

Just then, Raksha hobbled around Mary's car. Even in the darkness, the blood stood out on her fur, around her mouth, where, she'd bitten the intruder, and on her shoulder, where she'd been stabbed.

Valen was gripped with horror. "Raksha!" He ran to her and kneeled down, putting his hand on the bleeding wound. "Hang in there, girl."

"Is she gonna be okay?" Sam asked.

"Did she kill him?" Asked Mary.

Valen spoke solemnly, "This looks bad, I'm afraid. I don't know. We need to get her to a vet. Right away. And, no, she didn't kill him." He smiled sadly, as he petted his guardian. "Otherwise she'd have brought me his hand to show it."

"Well let's go then," Sam urged. "I'll drive. Mary's too shaken up."

"Fine with me," Mary allowed.

The four of them loaded into Mary's car, Sam at the wheel, Valen in the passenger seat, and Mary and Raksha in the back. Mary remembered feeling that she couldn't forgive Raksha, at one point, for frightening her. Now she hugged her with tremendous force, not wanting to let go of the beast who'd saved her life.

Valen was angry. The vampire killer had been something he could have done without in Nightfire, but now it had gotten personal. A line had been crossed. Valen promised himself, silently, that if Raksha bled to death, he would see to it that this serial killer died in prolonged agony. He muttered through clenched teeth, "I've had more than enough of this serial killer."

Ray didn't know what possessed him to go to church the following morning. Surely it wasn't God. He knew better than to believe in God. Maybe it was the people. The fellowshipping. He'd been with the Stevenses for two nights in a row, and he needed to get out of that house. It was too sad a place. He'd tried to get Bradley to come with him, but there was just no talking him into it.

Ray was very worried about Bradley. The younger man was clearly being swallowed up by a very bleak depression. Ray hoped it would pass, though he knew there was still so much to do before it could. The funeral had to be over and done with first. A plan for how the Stevens kids would survive had to be in place. In a way, Ray was grateful for something this epic to occupy his mind. At the same time, however, it was like a nightmare, and he couldn't wake up.

Ray heard not a word of Reverend Michaels' sermon. He was lost in his thoughts, and he was also scoping people out, picking familiar faces out of the crowd from when he and Donny had been in the church youth group. He saw Doris Gardner, and that led his eyes to the Preston sisters, Mati and Helen. What a trio they were, all dressed up in their Sunday best.

***

Helen Preston let out a gasp. *Oh my God! He's looking at me…and smiling!* Ray Don, the most beautiful man alive, had just smiled at her.

Doris and Mati both looked at Helen in unison. Helen turned and saw them staring. "What? Shit!"

Mati laughed harder than she would have liked to at this. "Shhh! Helen, we're in church." A fact of church was, things were always funnier, when you weren't supposed to be laughing; like while the preacher was wrapping up his sermon.

Helen started to laugh at her sister's laughing, but she didn't lose control. "Why were y'all staring at me?"

Doris told her teasingly, "Because, you have a thing for Ray. Because you wanna suck…his…dick."

Mati hid her face in a hymnal, laughing like a fool. She managed to wheeze, "Doris! Shut up! Church!"

Doris laughed wickedly, noting that Helen had turned bright, glowing red. "Mm-hm. Somebody's got a crush." She found it in her heart to sympathize. "Not that I blame you, Helen. He is *hot*!" She leaned over and whispered loudly in Helen's ear, "I wouldn't mind slurpin' some myself." At this point, convulsing with forbidden laughter, Mati got up and went to the bathroom.

Doris was very pleased with herself. "So, how long?"

Helen wasn't sure what Doris was asking. "How *long*?"

Doris slapped her shoulder playfully. "How long have you wanted his cock, you hornball?"

"Doris, it's not like that…I… *really* like him. Not just his body. He's just…always been my ideal man. Since I was a little girl."

Doris cackled. "Now you've got these hormones to contend with, and they will *murder* you, bitch! You want me to ask him for you?"

People were starting to turn around and glare at Doris, but Helen didn't care. They glared at Doris almost *every* Sunday. This time, though, Helen was getting things off her chest. Important things. And Doris was understanding her. "Ask him what?"

"If he'll show it to you."

"Doris! No!"

"Oh, c'mon, Helen. You've gotta lose it sometime."

Helen giggled. "Doris! You're the devil! I don't want to just get it on with Ray. I want to have a *relationship* with him. I'm serious. He's my dream guy."

"Oh, God! You are so retarded." Doris sat up straight and nodded. "I'll ask him for you."

"Whatever, Doris."

Mati made her way back to the pew. Doris looked at her with a smirk, and she started laughing again. Off to the bathroom.

The sermon ended, and people began filing out the doors, where Reverend Michaels was shaking each of their hands in turn. Ann made her way through the small crowd to Ray, who she'd spotted earlier. "Ray!"

Ray turned, surprised to see the lately elusive Annabelle Maryweather. "Ann. Nice of you to show up somewhere. Bradley's been trying to call you. I know he stopped, but, well, his mom died and all." Ray had decided not to like Ann. He knew she didn't care about Bradley.

"Yeah, I know. That's what I wanted to talk to you about."

"Oh yeah?"

"I was hoping you could tell him for me…not to call me anymore. Just tell him I'm not interested. I just…can't have a clingy boyfriend right now."

"Clingy?" Ray was pissed off. "Look you two-dollar hussy, if you wanna break Bradley's heart even more than it already is, do it yourself! I'm not your God damned messenger boy. It's not my fault you're a sniveling, cowardly psychotic. Bradley's the best thing you ever had. And breaking up with him, through your mother I might add, was the best gift you ever gave him."

Ann was in tears, and she ran out through the doors. Everyone was staring at Ray. He shrugged. "Well…it's true." To Ray's surprise, several of the spectators chimed in supporting his impromptu sermon to Ann.

"Was that Ann?" Doris asked Helen. "Where's she been?"

"See?" Helen said to Doris. "He's wonderful. He stands up for his friends without even blinking. He's so…charming!"

Doris rolled her eyes. "Oh, that's it. I'll go ask him for you." Doris started marching towards Ray.

"Doris no!" Helen ran and hid behind a group of chatty old people. She watched.

"Hey, Ray!" Doris shouted, as she approached him.

Ray smiled. "Doris. How's life?"

"Pretty good, gorgeous. How'd you get here this morning?"

"I borrowed Bradley's car."

"Ooh, you have wheels! I rode with Mati and *Helen*. Wanna give me a ride home then?"

He shrugged. "Sure."

"*Helen*, by the way, would love to know what kind of underwear you wear."

"Doris," he said, "you're so weird."

She linked arms with him and walked him out the door, saying, "I'm liberated, Ray! That's why we make such a great team. If we sat together in church, I'm *sure* that lightning would strike till there was no building left at all. And I'd be laughing in Hell."

Ray laughed as they walked away.

Helen stared, mortified, watching them leave together, arm in arm.

Valen Alexas approached the Stevens house apprehensively. He was so used to having Raksha with him that traveling without her made him nervous. He knocked on the door.

Bradley opened it. "Valen! Hi. I heard about what happened out at your place last night."

Valen showed his anger. "Yes, we had the police out...looking for clues. Of course, they found nothing. And my wolf is homebound until she heals. I'm just glad we got her to the vet in time. I get so attached to pets."

"So what brings you by?"

Valen smirked. "Well, I was restless mainly. Just walking. I wanted to see how you were doing since two nights ago. I was concerned for you."

"I'm all right. I mean... I'm getting by. The funeral's tomorrow."

"I hear Ray's staying with you."

"Yeah. He stepped out though. This morning, he had to go to church. Tonight, he had to get out."

"Why didn't you go with him?"

Bradley looked away. "I don't know. I'm...just not up to it."

"I understand. Bradley, I really just wanted to tell you again that I'll help you in any way I can. I want to help you, with the funeral expenses, if you'll let me. I think of you as a kindred spirit. We both are orphans."

Bradley was surprised, and relieved all at once. "I...yes! I mean, I don't really have a choice. Thank you."

Valen seemed satisfied. "Good. Well, I really must get back to Raksha. I don't like leaving her."

"Okay, well, stop by sometime when she's feeling better. Stay a while."

Valen smiled. "I'll do that, Bradley. Thank you." As Valen walked away, he felt warm inside. He was developing friends after all.

Ray sat at the bar at Dan Parker's. He was drinking nothing harder than a Dr. Pepper. His drink of choice. Once again, he'd just needed to get some fresh air. He heard a familiar voice behind him. "Hey, stranger."

Ray turned to see Doris. He smiled. "Long time, no see. What brings you by?"

"Nothing much. Just bored." She sat down beside him. "You know, Bradley's *ex*-girlfriend is a real psycho. I just called her and tried to talk to her about this morning, but she went crazy. She did the same shit to Jeffrey Mason a while back."

Ray was interested. "Really? What shit is that?"

"You know, she shagged him and dropped him basically. She's just weird. Now, she won't even talk to him if she has to say more than two words. The difference is, she actually had a wholesome relationship with Bradley for a while first. I don't get it. If I could have Bradley once, I'd have to have him more than once." She laughed. "She said some weird thing about moving to Boston."

Ray looked at her, confused. "Boston? What's in Boston?"

Doris rolled her eyes. "Who knows? She's crazy. Maybe she has some magical better friends who understand her mental abnormality there. It could be anything. I don't know. I stopped listening when she stopped making sense."

Ray hated Ann. "Do me a favor, Doris. Don't tell Bradley any of this. He *loved* Ann. Not that she deserved him. He doesn't need this shit right now. I should kill her for trying to make things worse this morning. God. I just can't believe her."

"I'll keep quiet, Ray." She smiled wickedly, which was her favorite way to smile. "Buy me a drink?"

Ray shrugged. "Sure."

Valen Alexas walked through the front door of his house. "Raksha! I'm home!" He turned on the living room lights. There was not a peep from his faithful wolf. "Raksha?"

He went to the kitchen and saw her lying on the floor, not responding to his calls. His heart skipped a beat. He rushed again to her side. Her bandages were in place, covering her stitches, so she wouldn't chew them off. He felt her throat. She was breathing. "Drugged." he whispered. He knew at that moment, he was not alone in the house. The serial killer had come back for his revenge. But why hadn't he killed Raksha?

Suddenly, something clicked. The killer could have gone for Raksha's throat the night before, but he didn't. He had no intention of killing her. There was wolf hair at the scene of every murder. Valen didn't know how he'd missed it until now. He stood. "I know you're in here. Stop hiding."

Then, from behind, a hand grabbed his mouth, and he felt something sharp at his throat, and a voice softly whispered, "Don't…" But Valen had no patience for this, and he was much stronger than the killer. He did a quick martial arts maneuver that he'd learned from his friend Julius, allowing him to escape from the killer's grip and flip the man over his shoulder, tossing him to the wall. Valen then fell on the man, grabbed his arm in a fury, and pulled the shoulder out of socket. He then twisted one of the killer's legs, until he heard it pop.

The killer screamed in agony. "Why don't you just kill me!"

Valen stood back and smiled. "Oh, I will. I just want to hurt you first. I want you to realize just how stupid you are." He looked at the man, who wore the skin of a red wolf over his head and along his back. The weapon he'd used was made of wolf teeth. He recognized this one as low ranking.

He went on. "I figured it out, when I knew that you wouldn't kill Raksha. Not the noble wolf. A werewolf acolyte only kills one wolf, to drink its blood and make a cloak, for initiation. I am here, because werewolves can't stand the stench of their own dead; which is why a vial of werewolf blood is kept in the basement of a local structure—to keep your masters out. Ah, but they can send an acolyte. A stupid acolyte. I'm going to send them one of your hands."

The man looked terrified. "Let me go. I'll tell them I killed you."

"I don't think so. I'm afraid you killed too many people attempting to frame me. You idiot. I'm going to kill you and place your body somewhere that won't implicate me at all. There's a great underground tunnel system here, and it's completely at my disposal. You see, when we founded Nightfire as a feeding ground in 1847, we knew we'd need a tunnel system to get around and hide ourselves and the bodies of our prey, so that no one would suspect us. Let you go? After all that you've done here? After you dared wound Raksha? After you murdered that poor boy's mother? After you tried to expose my presence? No. Never. You just picked the wrong vampire to mess with."

The man cried out, begged for mercy. Valentinus would hear none of it, as he silently went to work.

The Chronicles of Nightfire, Texas
will continue…

www.ingramcontent.com/pod-product-compliance
Lightning Source LLC
Chambersburg PA
CBHW020614310726
48979CB00008B/1484/J
9781618150868